S

Harry Mathews · Mark Polizzotti · Olivier Rolin · Sonia Greenlee · Jeannette · Jean Echenoz · Patrick Deville · Florence Delay

a novel

Lumen Editions & Alyscamps Press • 1997

This edition is published jointly by
LUMEN EDITIONS
a division of Brookline Books
P. O. Box 1047
Cambridge, Massachusetts 02238

and by

ALYSCAMPS PRESS
35, rue de l'Espérance
Paris 75013, France.

Compilation copyright © 1991 by Les Editions de Minuit
Translation of texts by Deville and Echenoz
copyright © 1997 by Mark Polizzotti
Translation of texts by Delay and Rolin
copyright © 1997 by Matthew Escobar

Originally published in French in 1991 as *Semaines de Suzanne*
by Editions de Minuit, Paris.

All rights reserved. No part of this work covered by the copyright hereon
may be reproduced or used in any form or by any means—graphic,
electronic, or mechanical, including photocopying, recording,
taping, or information storage and retrieval systems—
without the permission of the publisher.

Library of Congress Cataloging-in-Publication Information
Semaines de Suzanne. English
S. : a novel / Florence Delay ... [et al.].
p.   cm.
ISBN 1-57129-043-5 (pbk.)
I. Delay, Florence, 1941–   . II. Title.
PQ2679.E37513   1997
843'.914—DC21   97-2553 CIP

British Library Cataloging in Publication Data.
A cataloging record for this book is available from the British Library.

ISBN: 1-57129-043-5 (USA)
ISBN: 1897722-923 (UK)

First English-language edition, 1997
Printed in Canada

Contents

Hocus-Pocus *Patrick Deville* 3

It Pays to Have Friends *Jean Echenoz* 17

A Flash, Then Night *Olivier Rolin* 31

Anthropoetics *Mark Polizzotti* 43

Who Will Get Her? *Florence Delay* 55

Let Us Pray *Sonja Greenlee* 71

The Quevedo Cipher *Harry Mathews* 85

Hocus-Pocus
~~~~~~

When she threatened to tell her daddy everything if I didn't take her along, the digital defloration and all the rest, I turned out the light and hummed "Only You." (You'll have to make Papa disappear, said the thirteen-and-a-half-year-old magician, who probably figured I could turn her father into a frog with a wave of my magic wand.) I ran my lips along her thigh and planted a moist exclamation point on her knee. That Susie Fotopolis was no beginner when it came to counting her unhatched chickens.

Lying close against me under the sheets, and while I pursued my introduction to the prestidigitator's art (from delicate manipulations to discreet palmings), she confided the idea she'd had the day before in math class: with the Blue Anchor's cash box, the two of us could run away and presto, easy as pie. (She had magazine tastes, my Susie; she wanted to see Monaco.)

I turned the lamp back on to look at her face (Alice's blue eyes in the white rabbit's lens, under straight black bangs), then tried to explain that her plan, amusing as it was, I couldn't deny (howdy, Papa — abracadabra — hey, what's that frog doing in here? — go on, shoo, outside), was a very bad plan. (I was more at ease as a third-rate conjurer. I couldn't stand pain, whether inflicted or received, and this little peculiarity had earned me a stint in the brig six months before.) The mere disappearance of my dove every night tore me apart, especially since it left a few feathers behind each time, poor angel. For the rest, I pulled two or three playing cards from the sleeve of my tux, a ping-pong ball from an ear in the audience, spirited away in passing a bit of junk jewelry, brooch or bracelet, that I unloaded the next day, and *voilà*. I added that, if you asked me, the daily take of the Blue Anchor would just about buy us a tank of gas on the way out of Ostend. Nothing more. (The argument was effective, for Susie, still so young, knew precious little about the value of money.)

Actually, I suspected old Fotopolis was making a pile — sums whose disappearance wouldn't have entailed any calls to the police — but I had a hard time seeing myself as Prince Charming behind the wheel, my little fairy on my knees (Susie thought I was capable of turning coaches into pumpkins, motorcycle cops into crossing guards). She had fallen asleep against my shoulder, hugging her mechanical stuffed spider in her arms, and I brushed my fingers through her hair: I had promised that later on I'd take her to the local fair. I kissed her on the ear and turned out the light.

The most elementary arithmetic — thirteen plus thirty-five — would today make Susie forty-eight. And a half. Sometimes, out of pure spite or a vain attempt to make myself feel better, I imagine her filling out some Flemish kitchen, surrounded by ugly porcelain and polished copper, the radiantly plump spouse of the town mailman. But it's the furtive ghost of a raw-boned girl that my lips seek out every morning: my dry lips on the pillow; the yellow, trembling hands of the thin and solitary old rat I've become, in this flea-ridden furnished studio in Miami Beach (hands and lips come down on the bottle of tequila teetering on the stack of *Playboys*). Susie passed too quickly and too close to my life. Like the way my artillery manual during the Algerian War described the effects of windblast: the body is intact, showing neither bloodstains nor burn marks; inside everything is shattered, ground raw for the past thirty-five years.

It was the summer of '56 and very hot, in Ostend and everywhere else. On the morning of my arrival, old Fotopolis, standing behind his counter, had the weary but dignified look of a seal abandoned in the sunny parking lot of a shopping center (watching the yellow trailer of the feckless circus fade into the distance). He was oozing his bad cholesterol, which he mopped off his brow with a dishrag; his white shirt was glued to his armpits with grey sweat. He drew us two beers, pulled a pack of Barclay filters from a drawer:

"Let's see what you got."

I was used to such familiarity and stayed calm (I think Fotopolis reminded me a bit of Duval). At the Blue Anchor, he booked vaudeville artists who were fairly pathetic and very badly paid — trainers of hairless dogs, ventriloquists, charmers of inoffensive snakes — and he hired me for the week. Modest glory. The air reeked of stale cigarette smoke. I was standing

5

near the percolator in my raggedy tux, showing him a manipulation of Chinese linking rings, a bit of handkerchief-wand.

"That's good," he said. "It's classic."

That, it was. To his right, the sun was hitting the pattern of colored-glass diamonds, a promotional window for Leffe beer. Fotopolis set two fresh ones on our coasters, wiped cups, rubbed the rag over his neck. I lit a Barclay. Three beers later, he confided that he also organized a few hands of poker and blackjack, two evenings a week by invitation, in his apartment just above where I'd be staying. He asked if I would help him pluck certain pigeons of his acquaintance, fifty-fifty.

"You're on."

Why not?

That first evening, I kept my talents as a pickpocket in check — I wasn't very sure of myself at the time — to concentrate on my magic tricks. I hadn't touched a glass of alcohol all day and had even rehearsed, which didn't keep me from getting tangled up once again in the magic knot, presenting the rope to the audience three times in a row without the slightest modification. I'd fallen back on a smutty joke and had moved on to the foam balls. (I did some juggling to boot.) It was in the middle of the show that I saw Susie for the first time, a brunette in a red-and-black gypsy dress crossing the room while drinking a soda through a straw, smiling at me. (A foam ball, already jealous — *pop, pop* — went to start a new life under the piano.) I was in top form and had ended with my tap-dance number. Sitting in the front row, Susie laughed.

"What say tomorrow we forget about the tap-dancing? Like a good fellow," Fotopolis said later, laying a hand on my shoulder.

After closing, I stayed at the bar to have some green Izarras with Mickey, the pianist, a Hercules with the brain of a paramecium who told me his money woes. (I was trying to undo that fucking magic knot with my teeth, ended up cutting the rope with a knife.) He'd gotten himself nicked as an accomplice at the Ostend casino, little Mickey. Fotopolis had covered him, and now half his salary went to erasing his gambling debts. The primitive had calculated — with an abacus? counting sticks? — that he still had seven years to go, instead of disappearing into the woodwork right now. (I was full of good advice when it came to giving the slip.)

"Nah, they'd find me," said Mickey, shaking his fat head. "They'd find me."

I bummed a cigarette from him and searched my pockets for some matches, coming up instead with a deck of cards, an address book, dice, a thimble, a pair of bicycle pliers, and a chromo of Sacré-Coeur. He handed me his lighter.

"And yet, I could," he said. "I could do it. Got some friends who are heading off to Florida in a sailing boat, next week. It ain't like I don't have the chance."

I slipped the handsome silver lighter into my sleeve with all the rest, and asked him where one might find that boat.

"Plage du Petit-Nice," said Mickey. "The *Key Largo Queen.*"

It was exactly what I needed, an unregistered boat bound for Florida. I took the address book out again, copied down the name of the vessel, slid the pencil back into its leather sheath, and went up to my room where I found Susie sitting on the bed.

"Don't you have school tomorrow?"

She had found it too good, she said, all that magic; she wanted me to do some more tricks for her. I came up close, stretched out my left arm and spread my fingers in the air, hup!, while with my right I pulled a violet from her hair that I lightly ran across her lips. The first rule, I said, is to draw attention as far away as possible from where something's going to happen. (I'm always a little didactic after midnight.) She wanted to see my magic wand; I showed it to her, in its case. She also wanted to know why I didn't have a white rabbit.

"I used to have one."

I removed my jacket and flung my fake bow tie across the room. I lay down on the bed, hands joined behind my neck. She lay next to me. I told her about the death by boredom of the rabbit Duval. (We had just spent two months face-to-face in a cell at the military prison at Aïn-Beïda, in Algeria; I kept my fingers nimble ten hours a day by manipulating the cap from an orange Pschitt bottle.)

"Why Duval?"

"The name of a general. It was a bet."

She took my long white hand in her tanned mitts and caressed it softly, like an angel or a dove:

"It's beautiful."

She ran it over her face (kissed the fingertips), over her neck, over the areolas of her small breasts — Susie had quickly understood that I was the tactile sort — while I continued my story in a low voice (I felt her nipple stiffen and press against the hollow of my palm, now and again).

I had reached Tunisia under the tarp of a vegetable truck and traveled up through Italy in a night train, lifting a few wallets that I deposited the next day on the sticky desk of a garage, in the north of Marseilles. (The guy had seen others before, both deserters and wallets; his address was common knowledge throughout the interior and the casbah.) He took it all, the leather goods, cash, and papers, in exchange for a light-yellow Ford coupe pocked with rust, a whimsical registration card, and a wholly fictitious driver's license. While he typed my stage name — Felix Snoopes — and attached my photo, I discreetly recovered one wallet and relieved him of his Omega watch, just to keep my hand in. (A mechanic in an airman's blue overalls endowed the jalopy with fresh plates.)

I had sped toward Saint-Nazaire, where I expected to find Clara. Every hour the car radio played the same Platters song and I tapped along on the steering wheel, was still humming "Only You" as I bounded up the stairs with flowers in hand, stopped only when I compared my long, flat key with the two minuscule and very antipathetic locks lined up on the door of our apartment (no relation, any more than the name of the new tenant, Fernando Acosta — memory is a trash can — had with ours). Very early the next morning, in a bar in Petit-Maroc, her brother Clément informed me that my Clara had left France; that she had gone to live in Boston, rich and lighthearted, with the architect who had just recast the city in right angles.

Clément and I ate our croissants slowly and talked about the construction underway. Then the conversation had veered onto the war in general and aerial bombardments in particular. I told him a bit about Algeria, confided that thirteen and a half years earlier, in February '43, the pinwheels of burning phosphorus dancing over this very port, in the projector beams of the hurtling flak, had given me a taste for music halls and removed any I might have had for battle. (Clément hadn't seen a thing — too little.) An early-summer dawn in red and violet etched the outline of the submarine base on the café window, then that of the refrigeration shed; from the other side of the harbor basin, we heard the siren of the Atlantic Dockyards:

"Off to work we go," said Clément.

He wrote his sister's address on a notepad, tore off the sheet, and held out his hand.

"Bring her back, Felix."

He was a good guy, my brother-in-law. I reached Nantes that same afternoon, where I rented a magician's trunk and tux, and decided to follow the coast northward looking for engagements. Until I could find a boat for America, perhaps. For the moment, I'd gotten as far as Ostend.

"I'm going to sleep," said Susie. "Since you prefer old ladies."

It was true that she didn't have school the next day; it was Thursday. She spent the morning on a chair, watching me practice conjuring tricks and shuffle marked cards for that evening's round of poker. (The rest of the time she wound up her stuffed spider, put it gently on the floor, and let it scoot off in high gear.)

"What's she like, your Clara?"

"Tall. Blonde."

Susie shrugged her shoulders. I plucked the hair from my thumbs and the backs of my hands, coated them with talcum powder, then broke down a few tricks for her: sleight of hand, Italian grip.

"My mom's tall and blonde, too. Tall blondes always go away."

She didn't care much for her father, but she had come to live with him because here, she said, you could at least meet people. Sailors, performers. Her mother lived in the country, where she ran a pharmaceuticals lab. I spread sheets of sandpaper on the bed. I asked her to close her eyes and run the pulp of her fingers over the abrasive part, to put the numbers back in the right order. She had a fair amount of dexterity, that Susie, and finished the job in two shakes.

"At ease."

Then she asked me to close *my* eyes, took my hand and slid it between her legs. Her short tuft resisted gently under my seasoned fingers. I followed the wake of the index and put my left hand behind her neck, to bring her face closer to mine. She chewed at her lips while my middle finger caressed her smooth, warm membrane; I thrust in my ring finger and it tore; Susie bit me. Some trick. (She put a hand between her thighs and we kissed. We rolled slowly over the bed and the scattered sheets of sandpaper — I could do a decent fakir, too.)

"Hocus-pocus," she said.

A few evenings later, I quickly and unceremoniously swiped the security deposits of a local notary (the chrome ashtray routine, a piece of cake), and again found Susie sitting on my bed.

"I had an idea yesterday afternoon, in math class…"

Still, my disgrace would not be so complete if, to the stupid waste of the only bit of luck that life ever offered me, I wasn't forced to add the humiliation of never having been able, in those few days, to take Susie — if only once, if only from very far away and through binoculars — to see what she innocently dubbed the land of mischief. It made no difference that I could dissipate my keenest ardors with some clever manipulation: as soon as I was with her, as soon as I put my lips to hers and felt her tousle my hair, I found myself short of breath and standing on the teetering stool of the hanged man, the magic knot tight around my neck… Sitting cross-legged amid the rumpled sheets, she twisted the little key on the belly of her spider; docile, the animal stretched out its long, velvety legs. I could see that she harbored a certain disdain for human limitations, Susie — mine in particular.

I told her to get dressed: I was taking her to the fair in De Panne, as promised. (Hooray!) She threw on a burgundy polo shirt and beach shorts, we got into the dilapidated Ford and I headed south, in the direction of Oostduinkerke-Bad because I liked the name. The lavender-blue local shone on its rails and blockhouses sank imperceptibly into almond-green sea reeds; it was the middle of summer. The air rushing into the car made the deck of fifty-two dance on the dashboard (the queen of diamonds grazes Susie's smile, grumpily, and continues on her way); holiday-makers dressed in stripes sat at outdoor cafés nestled in the dunes. I bought two tokens at the booth — then pinched a dozen more to amuse Susie as they were handing me my change.

A fairly worthless colleague somehow managed to filch the Omega I'd kept for myself; a roving photographer handed me a shot of Susie and me from behind, shouldering up to shoot clay pigeons. That photo is here today, in my furnished room, one edge pinned between mirror and wall like an icon above the sink: the sole evidence of the last afternoon of my existence during which nothing, neither alcohol nor chemicals of any kind, helped move along the passing of the day... My lovely princess shivered in the tunnel of horrors (huddled against me in our lemon-yellow cart), shrieked with laughter on the Ferris wheel (in our strawberry-pink gondola), one hand brushing back her crazy hair and the other squeezing — no, no — the shiny chrome guardrail. I could see that when it came to the land of mischief, I was no match for even the plainest merry-go-round.

So today I'm this waxen specter in a long raincoat, who offers Chupa-chyps to the young Cuban girls of Little Havana and keeps away from the playground police. But that day, I bought Susie a vanilla-pistachio cone, some cotton candy, and a pair of sunglasses; then I took her back to Ostend. In front of the Blue Anchor, I told her I'd run out of cigarettes (kiss on the tip of her nose — five minutes, I promise), and I pushed on to the port, where I parked the car.

After having walked, suddenly indecisive, along the esplanade of the Petit-Nice and headed back up the landing dock, I crossed the gangplank of the *Key Largo Queen*. A man with greasy hair was painting a boom; another sitting on a wooden crate, red from the sun, was patching a sail; a third was busy with one of the other insignificant chores sailors do in port. "Easy, guys, I'm a friend of Mickey's." They followed me into the deckhouse. I nicely fanned out the notary's Belgian bills on the card table and made myself at home in a hammock. I had the distinct feeling that I'd win those bills back from them at 421 before this crossing was over. I also had a feeling that my desire to find Clara wasn't what it used to be.

I had a good first three years — my taste for Havanas satisfied — in the numerous casinos and cabarets that Cuba boasted at the time. I'd perfected a fairly salty knife-throwing routine with the help of a young Jungian with perfect measurements — 36, 25, 36 — who looked a little like Jean Harlow. We got a very good overview of the local nightclub scene, and it wasn't uncommon, back then, for the name of Felix Snoopes to shine in the firmament of the Tropicana, glimmer in the neon pediments of Cienfuegos. Then the revolution of '59 dropped us, she into the arms of a *barbudo*, me on the beach before the pink palaces of Miami, where I finally opted for pick pocketing. Uniting economy with larceny, handicapped by diminished reflexes, I now sit in bars sipping the few dollars I've managed to siphon from tourists. And now and then I send the postcard rack spinning with one finger, prop a card against my carafe and imagine sending it to you, Susie, while humming "Only You," or else songs that are just a little more recent — "Wake Up, Little Susie" or "Susie Q" — I know them all, Susie. I know every one.

— *translated by Mark Polizzotti*

It Pays to Have Friends
~~~~~~~

I TOLD THEM A HUNDRED TIMES I didn't bring the lye. Elmer found it in the kitchen with the other household products. The bandages and cotton wads were in the first-aid kit in the bathroom and the extension cord was around, too, in the living room, connecting the television to the outlet. Sue went to fetch the wire from the trunk of the car. As for me, I'll admit I filled the tub, but for the rest I wash my hands.

We'd met Sue a few weeks before, early fall at the seashore, just about when school was starting back up. Elmer and I wouldn't be starting back up with it, preferring to spend our time on the waterfront and in the bars. Near the port we'd gotten to know some Malayan, Senegalese, Latvian, and Breton sailors: rewarding encounters, since they don't teach those languages around here. A fair number of these new friends toasted and buttered their daily bread by dealing in natural or manufactured products — exotic, always interesting, sometimes intoxicating; it was all very educational. At first our offers to help carry and sell these products (we had a reliable little car on hand) were only accepted once in a while; sometimes they came to a sudden end, and now and then we were taken for a ride. But by holding steady, we ended up with an association that worked all around, and was more lucrative than the obscure trades our ex-school chums had set their sights on. So we had plenty of time to spend at the Cinévog, the Family, the Rex, and the Bijou, to watch the world at our leisure with its beaches and carriages, smoking Black Sobranies. It was on one of those free afternoons at the Petit-Nice that we came across Sue.

It's no lie that Elmer always found or decided things a few fractions of a second before me, so a casual observer could easily think he was in charge. Of course, it was nothing like that. It's just that he's impetuous by nature while I'm more reflective. And if we make such a good match, it's also because I've got (no argument there) more strength and physical resistance than he does. But the fact is, it was still Elmer who spotted Sue first.

She was with Lulu Swarczman and some young guy wearing brand-X jeans. Personally, I like Lulu Swarczman. She's every bit as tall and almost as broad as me; her voice isn't as high as mine; and we had some terrific fights together in the courtyard of our building when we were kids. The brand-X guy was busy telling the two girls about Confucius and Lao Tzu and other chumps of that sort who've written books I haven't gotten around to yet. While Lulu Swarczman and I exchanged manly hellos, I could immediately see that Elmer was interested in Sue, so it wouldn't be a bad thing for us to dump the mystic. When the mystic in question started in on Buddha, Elmer coldly stated that he didn't like Buddha. At that, the jerk made a show of pursing his lips and squaring his shoulders, but Elmer's opinion made Sue laugh out loud. We saw her pretty little canines, white and pointed, which she probably still has: the hardest part was over. Elmer laughed along with her, looking at her the way I know he knows how, so that the spiritualist got red in the face, then took a hike soon after. Elmer kissed Sue that same evening at the Family while Lulu and I watched the movie, then they continued in the back seat of the car while Lulu and I, in front, talked about the movie. Even so, from time to time I glanced back at them, casual as a clam, but after a while I couldn't see anything in the rearview mirror.

The next day we all met up on the beach, and from that point on we hardly left each other's sides until the business with Mesmaeker. Lulu Swarczman and Sue stayed in high school a few weeks more, but we soon had them seeing things our way. After that, the girls joined us in all our activities; soon they even started making themselves useful, especially Sue, who quickly proved to have good organization and management skills. As our profits rose, we rented two rooms not far from the port, on Passage du Contre-amiral Tlooth, which was fine by me given my mother's welcome when I got home at night. Since Elmer and Sue hardly left their room that first week, Lulu Swarczman and I had nothing better to do, so we followed along and slept together, too. It wasn't too different from when we used to fight in the courtyard. It brought back some nice memories.

Then we changed headquarters. Before, we'd mainly hung out at the Dovetail and the Neptunia, near the dry dock — popular spots with the passing seamen who were our main business partners — and then Sue introduced us to her father's bar: the man was repulsive, but his place was full of opportunities. We quickly realized that a secret gambling table attracted faithful regulars to the floor above, and we got chummy with a few of them. Fotopolis distrusted us at first, then he mellowed when we started showing up with cases of duty-free liquor and cigars. With the Blue Anchor as our base, we put in a few hours every morning, as sailors the world over came to consult us about the value of their goods on the fluctuating market. We judged, weighed, and tasted the things that we got rid of in the afternoon.

This kind of activity demands a vehicle in perfect working condition, so we kept the 2 CV in tip-top shape. The slightest breakdown, the smallest scratch gave us an excuse to sharpen our nail file, the ideal passkey for stealing any car of the same make, even from across the French border — after which we exchanged the faulty part: hood, engine, exhaust pipe, tires. Sometimes we'd bother to return the car to its parking spot, but at others it was more fun to burn or drown it, depending on our mood, in an abandoned lot or the water. I was partial to the North Sea; Elmer has always liked fire. Once, when we were a little annoyed from having waited in vain for some Ecuadorian cabin boy and the cash we'd left with him, we stole one just to change the floor mat, before bashing it in with crowbars — a way of calming down.

Sue's humors played on Elmer's emotions to the third or fourth power. He laughed too loud at her every smile, while her slightest frown plunged him in despair. And he became dangerous to himself and everyone else when she was in a mood, which wasn't rare. His jealousy was chronic, and retrospective: for instance, he took way too hard the story she told us of her deflowering by a traveling magician, whose supersonic copulation technique immediately earned him (thanks to us) the nickname Presto. The event dated from when the Blue Anchor used to host passing attractions, trainers of juggling rats or literate fleas, before Fotopolis ran into some problems with the labor authorities after an uninsured contorsionist got water on the knee in mid-performance. I'm kind of sorry not to have known that period, whose only remaining trace was a dim-witted pianist.

Elmer liked to pass the time upstairs, having made friends with some benign high-rollers: Angelo, Van Goethem, and especially Mesmaeker, who enjoyed privileged status among the intimates. A fairly nice guy, smart within reason, Mesmaeker lived idle and alone in a small house he'd inherited from his family, having also inherited enough capital to spend the rest of his life in relative ease. He spent a portion of his holdings and his Wednesday evenings on stud poker. After Sue's mother had left Sue's father, Mesmaeker had taken charge of raising Fotopolis's spirits, among other things seeing to it that the little girl, who had no one else to guide her, went to school regularly — the strange thing was, he never seemed angry at us for having cut her studies short with our bad influence. He also played the part of vague godfather, distant uncle, though I suspect Fotopolis was figuring on letting him have the girl someday for some kind of settlement. But I don't think Mesmaeker was in on that vile plan. If you ask me, he

S. ~~~~~~~~~~~~

had no ulterior motives when he showed an avuncular kindness toward Sue, gave her little presents or compliments, petted her head at the drop of a hat. Now, it's obviously not the same thing to touch the hair of a child, a young girl, a woman, or an old lady. It doesn't involve the same consequences. There are some big nuances that Mesmaeker didn't quite get, though he seemed to have had enough experience.

Whatever the case, big nuances and little presents ended up irritating Elmer, who at first had gotten along well with the bachelor. The gift of a star-shaped pendant in cheap gold plate — just a humble trinket, practically junk — pulled the stopper on his exasperation. We'll never know if his plan was due only to jealousy, or whether the cash that Mesmarker had, for once, won that Wednesday evening at Fotopolis's, played a part in Elmer's extreme impulsiveness. But the fact is, he decided to go give the other a piece of his mind.

Lulu and I weren't very keen on the idea, especially since through our private network we'd just gotten a huge TV set. I was looking forward to *Highway Patrol*, after which Lulu wouldn't have minded watching live coverage of Queen Juliana's visit. But Elmer insisted, arguing that we could watch this major event on Mesmaeker's even bigger, better, brand-new set. So we said okay; not all that happy, but okay.

As usual when he was worked up, Elmer let me drive. Not entirely sure this visit was for the best, I might have been a tad distracted, maybe a little inattentive, and I took two or three turns a bit less smoothly than I might have. Elmer, at his wits' end, made a few evil remarks about my abilities behind the wheel; I held back as long as I could, but we ended up quarrelling. In the back, the girls kept up contrasting silences: if the circumstances were right, Sue didn't mind putting on a cold indifference that she imagined made her look like Bonnie Parker; while Lulu, I could tell, kept hers shut because she was scared stiff. Once, trying to reassure her, I passed my hand behind the seat to pet one of her thick ankles, and that's when I almost missed the turn, and Elmer cast doubts on my driving skills, and we quarrelled, as I said. All the way to Mesmaeker's, the rest of the trip was silent as bronze.

I parked the car fifty yards from the house, having cut the lights a hundred yards before. We got out without slamming the doors, then moved closer. Lulu fearfully gripped my body as we circled round the dark building; there was no light peeking from the squares of closed blinds. Squatting at the entrance, Elmer pulled from his jacket several so-called passkeys he'd picked up here and there, but none of them could get the better of the heavy lock. When he repocketed his picks with some mortal blasphemies, I thought he'd given up, which would have relieved us no end. Already Lulu's nails were digging out of my forearm, and in a soothing voice I suggested we all go home. But as he inspected Mesmaeker's place one last time, Elmer spotted the small window of a bathroom or closet on the second floor, protected by no shutter. "There's our entrance," he muttered. "We'll get in that way."

I was quick to point out that the window was too tight for me, or Lulu, or even him, and he wasn't very broad-shouldered. He reluctantly agreed, and I breathed easy once more.

S. ~~~~~~~~~~~~

But I hadn't counted on the initiative of Sue, who whispered in the shadows that she could pass through with no problem if we lifted her to the opening. Elmer gave her a worried smile as he patted his clothes, handed her his glass-cutter; then, after a leg-up or two and some footholds on the gutter and the cornice, Sue managed to get a firm grip on the narrow window sill. From below, without being able to see much of anything, we heard the dry groan of the diamond on the pane, the brief shattering of glass like the tinkling of a triangle, then the creaks of the handle, the rusty hinges, and less than a minute later Sue opened the door for us. For a couple of seconds we stood lost in the unlit foyer — Lulu now had ten nails planted in my arm — then Sue whispered that Mesmaeker was asleep upstairs, the yellow door at the end of the hall. I could feel Elmer looking at her strangely in the dark, and I wondered myself how she'd managed to locate the bedroom so fast, but it wasn't really the time for exploring the question so we all tiptoed upstairs.

Once in front of the yellow door, Elmer took a deep breath, then bashed it in with a tremendous kick: a technique he'd no doubt picked up from a Felix Marten film at the Bijou three days before. Across the room there was an alarmed mumbling and a rustling of fabric, then a quick flash after the sound of a bedside lamp falling, the bulb having blown — then Elmer switched on the overhead light. Our friend Mesmaeker was all twisted up in his pale sheets and yellow pyjamas, rubbing his eyes amid stacks of magazines while asking in a squeaky voice what was going on. I was embarrassed to see him looking so frail, and turned away to read the titles of the scattered magazines, which all seemed to be fairly light reading.

Having found his glasses, Mesmaeker eventually recognized us and asked us again what was going on, what we wanted, what we were doing there, all in an ill-assured tone. In a voice that was none too assured, either, Elmer declared that he was sick and tired of Mesmaeker buzzing around Sue, that it was somehow offensive for her, humiliating for himself, and unacceptable for all of us, who had come to demand an apology, plus a small fine. After several more dumbfounded instants, the other finally started to get mad, with increasing volume and vulgarity; we who knew him slightly were amazed by his vocabulary. Then he clumsily told us to get out.

As if he'd been waiting just for that, Elmer informed Mesmaeker that he was, alas, in these conditions, forced to take a different tack. From one of his inexhaustible pockets he pulled a pretty cool hunting knife with laminated carbon steel blade, razor edge, biotechnological rosewood handle, and nickel trim: I'd never seen this item. Mesmaeker immediately stiffened like pudding, while his hollow voice guessed that we didn't know what we were doing and that no good would come of this, especially for us. Sure, said Elmer in a detached, preoccupied tone, sure — then he asked Sue to go get the spool of wire from the car.

When she returned, he explained once more to the bedridden man that everything could still be resolved in a friendly fashion, that all Mesmaeker had to do was hand over the results of his stud poker activities that evening and we'd remove ourselves from the premises; we required only the transfer of that small sum, which was ill-gotten to boot. But as patiently as Elmer made his case, fiddling with his neat knife all the while, the other didn't seem to want to hear. He started getting worked up again, raising his voice, so that Elmer finally handed me the wire and suggested I tie Mesmaeker to his bed. I thought about it a bit, then said no. Elmer seemed to ponder it as well, then said okay, all right, I'll take care of it myself, would you at least fill the bathtub for me.

"You sure you want to take a bath here?" I objected. "At this time of night?"

"I'm sure," he answered, beginning to foam. "It'll relax me. Can't you see how tense I am." So I motioned for Lulu to follow, and we went off in search of the bathroom.

We found some beauty products, which she took advantage of to redo her face. We grappled a little in our way in front of the mirror; I found her just right beneath the red lipstick, the blue eyeshadow. Back then I often encouraged her to cultivate her appearance, taking Sue as an example — then the latter burst into the bathroom like a torpedo, rifling through all the shelves until she found the cotton and adhesive bandages. "What's going on?" I asked. "Did someone get hurt?" — but she left without answering, and Lulu pulled me back into her arms. So I let her have her way a bit before remembering that show I wanted to catch.

A little bigger but no better than ours, just encased in a special cabinet, Mesmaeker's television sat in the living room on the ground floor. We made ourselves at home and turned the volume up full to drown out the noise the others were making upstairs; Lulu kept hanging on my neck. A short while later, Elmer crossed the living room toward the kitchen, still holding his pretty cool knife. I heard him rummaging in the cupboards, then saw him return with a little green container dangling from his arm, a container like any other, I've said a hundred times I didn't recognize it. Elmer wanted to know if we'd seen any electrical wire lying around, an extension cord or something; we answered evasively. Spotting the TV extension, he decisively unplugged it in spite of our protests, then walked away while stripping the female end. To see the rest of the show, Lulu and I had to drag the cabinet closer to the wall socket, then fifteen minutes later Elmer came back down during the closing credits, tenser than ever. Imperiously, he told me to come upstairs with him for a moment. So I followed him into the bathroom, where I saw that our troubles were just beginning.

Mesmaeker's bound bulk was two-thirds submerged in the tub, his adhesive gag partly unstuck like an old bandaid in the rain. It seemed to me he wasn't breathing much, which I tested with a little mirror, and his heart didn't seem to be beating much, either. When I wanted to know about those marks all over his body, Elmer shrugged and waved at the extension cord and container of lye. When I asked if Mesmaeker had finally said where the money was, he shrugged again and pulled a face. And when I finally expressed concern over Sue's absence, he turned around to notice that she was no longer there. But we found her soon afterward in the living room, with Lulu, in front of a special report on the visit of Their Majesties the King and Queen to Paris.

The hours that followed were the hardest. While the girls wound Mesmaeker in a sheet, we had to go find another car — and it's always the same story: those 2 CV's jammed every street of Western Europe at the time, but all you had to do was really need one and they were nowhere to be found. Then the one we finally got our hands on didn't have enough gas, so we had to siphon some from another tank, and God knows I hate the taste of high octane, that inevitable swallow when starting the suction.

We returned to Mesmaeker's where the girls were waiting for us, watching over the corpse in his shroud and chugging his gin. Once I'd finally convinced Elmer not to burn the house down, we grabbed some resale items and the few bills we found in Mesmaeker's wallet, plus a little change from the right front pocket of his pants. His body we loaded into the new car, which I drove. Elmer and the girls got into ours, then they followed me to a pier I knew, where the water stays deep no matter what the tide. We plunged the car in with Mesmaeker inside, then watched the bubbles rise.

By then it was six, seven in the morning, and we weren't especially sleepy. I suggested we go try to eat something in Middelkerke-Bad, and so we headed that way. In Middelkerke-Bad at that hour, a kind of bar that served beer and seafood was still open. The seafood looked good, but first we counted our funds: with the slave's wages we'd swiped from Mesmaeker, no way to afford lobster and oysters. We made do with spider crab, cursing out the niggardly corpse. After an endless return trip to Passage du Contre-amiral Tlooth, we immediately went to bed, vaguely awoke in lousy shape before noon, then fell back asleep, and finally got up when it was already dark, like it was just a continuation of that same miserable night. After we'd glanced at each other with little affection, I was the first to say I was going home. I'll spare you the details of my mother's welcome.

Following this business, Elmer and I agreed not to see each other for a while, but I learned that he'd tried to see Sue, that he'd gone back once to the Blue Anchor: when he asked for a shandy — politely, mind you — Fotopolis pulled a pump-action shotgun from under the dish tub, and Elmer neither saw Sue nor drank his shandy. Maybe she was at her mother's. For the moment, I preferred to stay with mine, too; then I almost ran into Lulu Swarczman the second time I left the house, but her automatic change of sidewalk told me all I needed to know about the state of our love affair. I didn't have much to do with my time, no longer saw any foreign sailors. If I balked at the idea of going back to school, I didn't put up too much fuss when my mother told me about the apprenticeship contract with Doormise.

I was going to say yes, since I almost never saw Elmer anymore. The last time was when he'd gotten his hands on twelve grams of excellent pink heroin from a Madagascan coal trimmer. Within days he'd put half of it up his nose and given me a little; then, having cut the rest with detergent, he hit on the idea of selling it in a student bar, which normally catered to a reliable clientele. Of course, the first two students Elmer offered his powder to were plainclothes cops, and without further ado he got eight months.

He must have let something slip, unless the police managed all by themselves, but in any case they came to get me two weeks after his interrogation. Honorable to the last, we took full responsibility for the affair; not once during the trial were the girls' names mentioned. I made some good friends and got to know some specialized tradesmen in the fifteen years that followed. At the end of my sentence, as I left the prison, I met others who were heading in; they're probably still there today. I wonder if they'll have a special menu to ring in the new century.

— translated by Mark Polizzotti

A Flash, Then Night
~~~~~~~

Si mis P*ÁRPADOS, LISI, LABIOS FUERAN...* I have long since left those shores behind. My eyelids no longer suffer the misfortune of not being lips. My eyes no longer follow each woman's gait, her mouth, anything... Nothing is left. My hands are old and brittle. They dream no more. My lips speak little and in low tones. One would expect the body's rest to be accompanied by that of the soul. But that is not the case. Exhaustion has come instead. *Polvo serán, mas polvo enamorado.* I shall be turned to amorous dust. I recall every detail. I put myself into the hands of my Judge. I will never forget that night of November 1969 when, in the library–smoking parlor of the Medina-Schmidt palace, I read the *Sonnets to Lisi* by Quevedo. *Y en público, secretos, los amores...* It must have been one in the morning when the Señora signaled me to stop reading. I gathered up the pages and put them back in the fine cedar box, I placed the box on the small table between the two armchairs and sat back down on my stool. As often as I had made those simple movements, it now seemed to me that I was doing them for the last time. Miller took a Vuelta Abajo from his pocket, reached out and grasped a bundle of poems from the box, then crumpled and set them on fire to light the tip of his Havana cigar. Out of anger or disdain? The Señora's lips curled into a frown, those lips which Góngora would perhaps have turned into the waves toying with a shipwrecked man or a bow shooting the fatal arrow, and which in any case stirred up the most prosaic turmoil in me whenever I fantasized about nibbling on them, as I was doing at that very moment. Yes, I must confess that this was one of the many despicable thoughts I kept to myself. She lay her incredibly delicate wrists and hands on the armrests. How often had my mistress' miraculous hands, on the steering wheel (the hub of which was decorated with a flashing picture of Michelangelo's *Pietà*) of the Dodge truck in which we brought the merchandise back from the harbor, or grasping the stem of a champagne flute as one might pluck a delicate flower or raise a chalice, or else slapping an impudent worker who occasionally was me — how many times had they called to my deranged mind the blurry image of my Lord, the Crucified? Or should I say my former Lord? I was just a priest who had cast aside his belief, a defrocked Jesuit whom the kids of Vera Cruz followed down the street with jeers and obscene gestures. The voluptuousness of the Menéndez blood, which I thought I had smothered by donning the black robes of the *Compañía* at a young age and by taking the terrible oath of obedience to my teacher Ignatius, had not left me in peace for long. After the public revelations, notably in some intensely anticlerical papers, of my pathetic fornication with several barmaids and laundresses had spread my order's disgrace far beyond our national borders, I was ejected from the ranks of Christ's soldiers. It was at this point, in a *cantina* run by one of the creatures who had originally

A Flash, Then Night

tempted me, that I had met Miller, the same Miller who was now watching or not watching (it was impossible to say, so full were his blue-rimmed eyes of the stupidity that one could observe in the dead birds which a fetid backwash deposited on the escarpments and very foothills of the palace) his wife's hands tightly gripping the green silk armrests of her day bed. A brilliant diamond in the small spider-shaped pendant, which she always wore against her breast (even when she drove the truck or directed the unloading of the boats), caught, intensified, and blazed with the rare light that murkily shone throughout the dilapidated room containing all that our work had left intact of the thousands of books amassed by generations of Medina-Schmidts — generals, viceroys, bishops: all violent and depraved men, one of whom, convicted of buggery and bestiality, had been led by the *caballería mayor* (the final protection that one of his cousins, a prelate, had offered him, thus sparing him the humiliation of the donkey) to the nobleman's garrote erected on the city's central plaza; and of course, if that one man had been caught and tried in the end, it was because they said too often that many others before him had escaped the same ignominious death simply by virtue of their position in society or their money — the products of two abominably inbred branches of the same brutish, diseased family of *conquistadores* and lowlife Flemish soldiers who served under the Duke of Alba, and who considered books nothing more than another item to go along with their sumptuous wardrobe, incapable as they all were, the clerics included, of reading any further than the words *Credo in unum*

S. ~~~~~~~~~~~~

Deum. A brilliant burst of fire passed before my eyes and immediately called to my mind certain paintings of spectacular conversions, those of Paul of Tarsus or of Ignatius Loyola himself, my master, mixed in with several pious representations of the arrows with which the Lord likes to riddle his servants — and even more so, it seems to me, his lovers. All of this formed nothing more, to tell the truth, than a vague series of images — among which still echoed those "proud luminous-skinned wildcats" of which the previously read poetry spoke and the "Portrait of Lisi that he wore in a ring" — of crumpled, falling bodies and ghastly, shining, ferocious flesh. A *cucaracha*, a cockroach, slanting, precise in its zigzagging movement, crossed the rug, pulling me out of my fleeting reverie. I thought I could see the insect's eyes gleam, and all at once everything — how to explain it except by some electric flux in the atmosphere caused by the nearness of the hurricane, which as meteorological luck would have it bore the same name as the Señora: Susana — became both blurry and remarkably clear: like the veneer on an engraving whose relief had been nearly obliterated over time, without blurring the minute sureness of the features. Everything was thrown into shadow: the bookshelves, the sea that an ashen mist carried on feeble winds erased past the tall cracked windows; and yet each object seemed to possess the vivid clarity of a pearl. The torch of sonnets on the little table finally burnt itself out. Was it just a hallucination? I thought I saw small copper flames dance on the telescope used by who knows which Medina during the second siege of Cartagena de Indias, and through which Miller and the Señora watched the arrival at port of the *Espiritu Santo* and the *Nuestra Señora del Carmen*, the two old lobster boats that made the connection with Cuba for them. Miller, whose reputation among the port's thugs wasn't an enviable one, to say the least — wasn't there a story that he had accepted a shipment of crates containing Soviet Volga shock absorbers instead of a cargo of *kalashnikovs* meant for Colombian revolutionaries? — had recruited me for bookstore duty. I say "bookstore duty," but in reality that was only the technical, or dare I say distinguished, side of my work, which also consisted in cooking and serving the food. My humiliation would not have been complete, however, had the Señora not insisted, whether on a whim or out of pure cruelty, that I carry out my servile tasks in the robes I had dishonored. However, all insults seemed sweet so long as they came from her, and at other times, on the contrary, I saw in them the hard work necessary for my redemption: an exhausting, circular mechanism by which all carnal thoughts canceled out the movement of the soul, and that in turn caused me to loath what my sinful flesh, just an instant before, had given itself over to in adoration. The Señora slid her legs over to one side — my side — and I was unable to restrain myself from stealing a quick glance at her knees, which were left exposed by the hem of her black skirt. El Griego, her father, was rolling the dice at the back of the room across from the windows. That was how the old fool spent his nights when he wasn't on his rounds in the United States, charged with finding subscribers for the bookstore among the rich Greek immigrants. He and I were divided by a feeling of hatred — of a particularly vigilant sort, as we had each been separately directed not to let it show — that I believe stemmed from the fact that our desires secretly centered on the same object. The Señora put her foot on the rug speckled with a constellation of burns and cockroach stains and leaned forward. Once more I was unable to restrain my eyes from wandering, *si mis párpados labios fueran*. I would like to think that the reason for this was the curious phenomenon I just mentioned, the blurry precision each thing had, which I attributed to the imminence of the eponymous meteor. She was wearing a black bodice cut into a low V. ¡*Dios mio!* Is this what Mary Magdalene looked like? One could hear only the ivory clacking, and with each passing minute came a wailing similar to that of a foghorn, along with a movement in the air, like a sort of invisible wave. Miller smoked on. Hadn't he seen anything? The primitive nature of his genius would never have enabled him to set up the bookstore's activities. *She* was the one who thought the whole thing up, and she especially who had recruited my idle mind, so accustomed to books as it was, to write the catalogue that we sent to our subscribers in the United States. This way everything went according to the rules and the orders were placed and filled in the simplest, most legal manner in the world. The format, volume and number of pages specified allowed us to determine exactly what quantity, type and grade of cigar to send, the prices for which climbed ever higher since the American government had outlawed their importation. My mistress was standing now. She was the kind of woman whose

A Flash, Then Night

smallness showed off her perfect shape, like those wooden or ivory statuettes decorating certain holy coffers and reliquaries, that one can pick up and caress in the palm of one's hand and which are more moving than the stone Virgins high above in the nave upon which one's eyes wander aimlessly. Alas, I have always liked small women, so much so that some scribblers added insult to injury by daring to write that this made them easier to hide under my cassock. Using a stamping press with different dies corresponding to the folio, quarto and octavo sizes, we cut out the insides of the books we took from the immense library, leaving only the four outer edges intact. We then glued the pages together and stuffed cigars in the empty carcasses of *Don Quixote*, the *Lazarillo de Tormes*, the *Autos Sacramentales* by Calderón, as well as the *Book of Liberal Invention and the Art of Chess* by Ruy López de Segura, the *Ars Magna* by Ramón Lull, as well as *The Safe Way to Navigate the Rivers and Streams of the New World* by Lázaro Enrique Ahogado, the *The Appropriate Cuisine to Serve Daughters of Gentlemen in the New World* by Fray Francisco Esteban de la Sombra, the complete plays of Lope de Vega, the *Poems Martial and Galant* by General Osvaldo Bigotudo de la Cruz, mixed in with all the greater and lesser masters of antiquity, Dioscoridus, Theopompus, Callicles of Pergam, Plato, Denis of Halicarnasse, and a mountain of works in German, Italian, and French that the Medina-Schmidt family had taken from the spoils of the ephemeral Maximilian after his disastrous end. The Señora was standing there smoothing out her skirt over her hips, a gesture that I believe expressed no more than a

S. ~~~~~~~~~~~~

certain hesitation on her part; but I can no better describe the dreadful seductive effect it had on me than to say that, with my arms folded across my chest, I squeezed my hands against my sides as if to break them, possessed by a ferocious desire, so much did I fear that they would detach themselves from my wrists and fly over to unite with her slow white hands resting on the black silk. She took a *panatela* from the little table, raised it to her lips and, apparently changing her mind, broke it in two. Miller raised an eyebrow. He was a quiet man, possibly due to the stutter with which he was afflicted. At first we got rid of the printed pages we cut out by burning them in the large fireplace along with the cigar boxes, but, on the day when I had to throw the *Spiritual Exercises* into the flames, the shame I felt at betraying my teacher and my order drove me to remark to the Señora that lighting huge fires every day, when the sticky heat of the tropical summer weighed down on the streets of Vera Cruz, was bizarre enough to risk unnecessarily attracting the attention of our neighbors. She agreed, and we then began stuffing the pages into the Cohiba, Monte Cristo, or Carl Upmann boxes we had previously relieved of their contents. Then we would stack them on the shelves as fast as we emptied them. It was, I think, the perverse love I continued to feel for books that drove me to inscribe the side of each box with the title of the work it contained, so that the library we were rapidly creating north of the Rio Grande, with its false outward appearance hiding the exquisite Vuelta Abajo leaves, continued to exist here behind the façade of cigar boxes. Then something began to change in my mistress's fanciful mind.

A Flash, Then Night

Have I mentioned the rings under her eyes, which invited one to make a slip of the finger or tongue? Have I mentioned the color of those eyes, like a corrupted blue-green shadow? Have I mentioned her hair, of a blackness that swarmed with glimmering flames and metals, strands of which I saw (pulled back in a knot) beat rhythmically against her neck as she walked, beneath her ears, on that crescent of tender skin where mouths long to alight? — but I have mentioned nothing, so badly have the words that attracted me to her betrayed me when I wanted to use them to speak of her: perhaps, may God forgive me, that is what hell is? The care I took in placing the pages into their little wooden tabernacles finally aroused her curiosity over what she had originally seen as a simple expedient. One day she asked me, no doubt in mockery, to read her the trembling pages I held in my hands, the words on my lips. It was shortly following the death, mere days after its birth, of the only child she ever had with Miller. She was in mourning, and while I do not think it affected her deeply, it did incline her imperious personality toward a certain dreaminess, and distanced her from a man who was not worthy of her. After that first reading others followed, more and more regularly. What had begun as nothing more than a game or a form of relaxation became a habit, and soon after, a passion. This progressive possession was, I dare say, entirely of my own devising. I evolved the desperate plan to dominate her through books. I chose the works that I would read to her with the maniacal care of a magician preparing a potion, adding in and mixing the desired effects of fear, desire, suspense, happiness, surprise, and lascivious or terrible imaginings, following the progress I could discern in her soul, taking into account as well the times of day when she would call me to her side. For example, I would not read the same pages, nor would I read them in the same way, when the sparkling midday sun slid its oblique rays through the blinds and along her outstretched body, while the breeze from the fans bulged and lifted up the pages in their box like something alive and shivering; and when the night's fresh air brought with it the sea's mist from down below and drove the great sacred Zapoteca bats from the eaves. Nor had I tonight, when the hurricane was erecting its walls and towers of vacuum, when I saw the serpentine muscles of her legs, thighs, and buttocks glide beneath her skin, then beneath her second skin of silk, as she walked toward the small mahogany desk with a confident step: neither the choice of that brigand Quevedo, nor the tone of my voice reading his sonnets, had been left to chance. El Griego stopped rolling the dice. Did he know what was in the lower left-hand drawer? One could hear far off a few incongruous notes played on the accordion. My mistress's new passion had slowly turned her attention away from the bookstore's activities. In order for her to find the clandestine business interesting, it would now have to be a story out of a book. Miller himself, who would have interested her had he been a character in a novel, each day grew too sordidly real, too concerned with the banal task of following through on the upkeep of the business which at this point he absurdly claimed as his own creation. The conflicts between them grew more frequent, and I naturally did my best to exacerbate them by

A Flash, Then Night

choosing just the right text at the right time to sharpen the feelings of disgust and fierce revolt that I could see in her. This new tension was never more evident than when (out of carelessness, but certainly out of a desire to ruffle her as well, like the pages I had just read her which, stupid as he was, he must nonetheless have recognized as subversive) he pretended to light his cigar after having set them on fire. My mistress was standing in front of the desk, leaning over it slightly. This movement made her thighs stick out and revealed the pale backs of her knees. A sort of low murmur could be heard beyond the windows. There is a man sleeping, an enormous one, just outside, I said to myself. El Griego stood at the other end of the room, stupidly looking at the dice. Sweat beaded on his forehead. Sitting there on my stool, I held my hands under my armpits, pressed them hard against my sides. A white flash — it was her hand — disturbed the dark mirror of the mahogany. Miller smoked on with his head tilted back. In my right palm I felt the pulse of my frenzied heartbeats. The smoke was forming a stiff blue column above Miller which broke far above him into arabesques, just before reaching the shadows. It looked as though a tree were growing out of his mouth. She opened the lower left-hand drawer and thrust her hand deep inside. A black bra strap appeared on her shoulder, revealed by the sliding silk. Then, as if by a pact with the devil she held in her fingers the invisible strings of the winds; as if the weapon she was about to seize, which I was now certain she would seize, were not some greasy, practical steel-grey tool, such as the hoodlums on the docks keep in their belts, but —

S. ~~~~~~~~~~~~~~

miraculously hidden in the narrow wooden case like the limitless revolution of literature in our deceptive boxes — the seething of the sea and air; or rather, as if the small mechanical cylinder that hands out dirty death and that, in the *cantinas* I frequented, was called the "mill of sudden death," were in her hand the metaphor, insignia, or symbol of that great merry-go-round of nothingness, the windows, against which a suddenly furious sea pressed its white crests like an approaching forest, shattered all at once, and then before the shards of glass had fallen, came — against the library, the palace, the entire city of Vera Cruz, and she and us and that incomprehensible thing between us, and our eyes in which the uprooted tree of lightning still burned — the brutal, crushing night.

— translated by Matthew Escobar

Anthropoetics

In the end, It was Claire who requested the divorce. Bowing to the expectations conferred by my rising young status, and not unmindful of a lifestyle that owed more to my future in-laws' prominence in local financial circles than to my projected renown in anthropological ones, I had led Claire down the aisle in my mid-twenties, and had then proceeded to layer for her a life as methodically dry as a mattress of lint. Our affection was fostered by mutual ignorance, reinforced by benign self-absorption on my part, on hers a sated and impregnable resistance to imagination. The fact was, this lack of imagination served me well. Claire felt no compulsion to ask questions, which in turn absolved me from the tedious invention of excuse. The money her trust fund had provided in the intervening decade and a half seemed to be all the response our silent exchanges demanded. And my own, more telling needs were easily assuaged by several women in several cities, whose banality dispensed with further comment.

But Claire's request had nothing to do with all that...

I still don't know how Suzanne happened to be at the party, to which I was condemned in solo by another of Claire's prolonged visits to one of her family's out-of-town bunkers. Across the table at which I found myself, she appeared to be conducting a series of interviews by turns with her fellow diners (accent on fellow), either filing their c.v.'s for future reference or dropping them into oblivion the moment the applicant quit the room. My answers must have satisfied her requirements.

"I want you to leave her." She had tipped her hand in the South, on a beach unseasonably mild for October. Suzanne disputed with the sea breeze the right to char-broil a cigarette, her ninth in less than two hours (nonsmoker's count). A small dune formed an imperfect barrier between us and the scattered couples, the abandoned families taking last advantage. The weary ocean fauna plumbed their instincts for hints on how to discourage these overstaying visitors from another genus.

I told her that leaving Claire would be impossible. And that, besides, the minute I was free she'd lose all interest. Suzanne looked at me, hard, then removed her suit without a word. I glanced worriedly at the bathers beyond the sandy partition. "Don't your wants *ever* get the better of you?" she said after a moment.

Suzanne used sex as torture and as persuasion, a logic that twisted everything into curlicues of meaning. I exhausted my erotic vocabulary trying to impress her: we made love on the linens, copulated in the car, rutted on the rug, fornicated on the furniture. It was simple as ABC — and, somehow, no more satisfying.

"I want you to leave her," she said again. We were sitting before our glasses at a dark table. I gave her some conventional reasoning and Suzanne, exasperated, left the bar. She knocked on the door of our room the next morning, tense, tired, proud. We arrived back in the city that evening. Claire was not at home.

I had met Fahrenheit only once or twice, but our relations had not lacked intellectual sympathy. He was the rage among certain youth, the most avant of the young literary guard. His excruciatingly compact poems had won him a select group of followers, whose numerical restraint was matched only by the intensity of their devotion. Shortly after our return from the South, Fahrenheit phoned about a project that "one of his people" had dreamed up, something he called "anthropoetics," and about which he seemed to want a few moments of my professional insight. "My elevated Schmidt," Fahrenheit breathed into the phone, "it will be supernal to revise you." We agreed to meet in three days' time at the Blue Ribbon, a pseudo-Irish pub he favored for his mandatory afternoon caucuses. "He's a brilliant discovery," the master sighed over the prize disciple. "He derives all his ideas from me."

Fahrenheit, surrounded by about twenty identically feverish young men, lifted his bulk as I entered with Suzanne and, when I introduced them, tilted it ceremoniously in her direction. "Suzanne!" he exclaimed. "'My wife with her forest-fire hair' — to borrow from the Ancients." The afternoon wore on: I answered a prolonged barrage of questions from the round, while Fahrenheit's interest veered increasingly toward Suzanne, whom he rebaptized Suze. We left after several hours

S. ~~~~~~~~~~

of exhaustive talk; after I had tried standing up three times; after I thought I glimpsed "Suze" pass Fahrenheit a slip of paper.

I saw nothing of Suzanne in the following days, nor was I successful in my attempts to find her. With forced nonchalance, I made roundabout inquiries of anyone who might have information, but no one — not even the hosts of the dinner at which we'd met — seemed to know anything about her. One morning about a week later, a note arrived at the door:

"My egregious $S^c{}_h{}^m{}_i{}^d{}_t$! If two heads are better than one, the other will surely roll. No refuge for the sick, no home underanged. Beware death by boredom."

I cancelled my afternoon lecture halfway through and went to the Blue Ribbon, but evening fell with no trace of Fahrenheit or his circle. Or Suzanne.

Several days afterward, a voice on the phone said what sounded like "Thickened version's fine," but which I soon realized was "The Conversions at five."

At the precise hour I arrived in front of the establishment, which stood in the part of town opposite the Blue Ribbon. I recognized Koos as the original "anthropoet." He leaned closer and, in conspiratorial tones, murmured that Fahrenheit had had… — but here his voice was buried by a simultaneous crash of plates. Around the bar I noticed faces watching us like proprietary dogs; I thought I recognized some of them from my meeting with the poet and his circle nearly two weeks earlier. "...a new order," Koos continued obscurely. "Fahrenheit is but an old grey hare and will be skinned as such. His standing drops with every grade. Mark my words, Schmidt, the future is in metrics."

Koos explained that some of Fahrenheit's followers had become disenchanted with certain reactionary elements of their leader's current outlook. For the past few weeks, they had been secretly working to build a radical dissident faction, of which he, Koos, would be the head. He also began to mutter something about "that woman...," stopped short, reddened, then abruptly confirmed that Suzanne and Fahrenheit were together somewhere in the city, without specifying where. "It will not be long," he blurted as he rose to leave, although whether he was referring to Fahrenheit's literary status, his idyll with Suzanne, or the eventual revelation of their whereabouts, I couldn't say.

When I was little, I used to watch my feet walking: one, two, one, two, so intently that at times I'd march into a tree or oncoming stroller. No matter: what interested me was the regularity of the steps themselves — one, two, to the end of the block, to the end of my studies, to the end...

It seemed I'd shown promise once, and back then I'd set out full of virtuous vim, ready to fulfill it with all the energy I could devise. The trouble was, things came easily. Women liked me; department chairmen liked me; Claire and her very comfortable family liked me. And now here I was, perhaps deriving little satisfaction from the rote recital of my anthropological insights, fresh only a decade ago, but, again, no matter: ease came easily, thanks to the strange durability of my old reputation, thanks also to Claire and her relative prosperity. And all I'd given in return was my hunger and my edge, sated and dulled by fifteen years of vegetative life. Somewhere along the way, my prized self-possession had come to resemble basic inertia.

The telephone rang. An hour later, in a bar across town, I told Suzanne she was looking tired.

"Fahrenheit and his bloody cocaine. He does twenty lines a day," she said, snapping the match that flared before her Chesterfield. "He was wearing me out. You're more restful." It was not exactly the tender remorse I'd been anticipating; still, when she mentioned a hotel, I put up little objection.

"You're going to cost me everything," I said.

"You'll get your money's worth," she replied.

During our time at the hotel, I gradually pieced together fragments of a story that she reluctantly, sometimes inadvertantly, provided. She had been rich: that much I could gather. Somewhere in the last few years she had lost her fortune, a little to various casinos, a little to displacements, but mostly to the acquisition of books whose rarity and costliness increased as her funds diminished. It was almost a compulsion, even when her reserves had touched bottom, and I thought of the look that would cross her face each time we passed a rare book dealer's.

But there were other aspects of her past that remained elusive, no matter how I tried to grasp them. Where did she come from? What was her background, her childhood? Silence. Silence, too, or close to it, on the men in her past. Suzanne had been married twice, it seemed: first, briefly, when she was a teenager, then to the Miller whose name she still wore, and with whom she'd apparently spent time in Mexico. (My last trip there, I couldn't help remembering, had been with Claire in the late sixties, during one of our few periods of domestic contentment. Actually, "contentment" is an exaggeration: Claire had been chronically dissatisfied, the beaches were mediocre, the food worse, and I'd had to leave Vera Cruz without seeing the fabulous Palacio Medina-Schmidt — an ancestor, I wondered? — because of an oncoming hurricane.) But as to details on the nature and duration of her marriages, or on the corresponding husbands, or any men in between, nil. What had put an end to these unions? What had happened to these men? Was Suzanne the Gay Divorcee? the Black Widow?

And despite all of it, I found myself wondering if I should do what she had asked. If I left Claire, married Suzanne, would it give me back some of the peace that these last weeks had crumpled? Would it restore some of the nuance that previous decades had so painstakingly ironed out? I knew it was the purest insanity to indulge in such fantasies. But there were moments when Suzanne would lean against me and, as if to herself, whisper that she was tired, or nothing at all. At those moments, things seemed to take on a logic of their own.

We spent two weeks at the hotel, then Suzanne decided on a train trip for us, made the arrangements (more cancelled lectures). I was reluctant at first, but quickly began to relish the idea of a brief vacation. No sooner had we arrived at the station platform, however, than the portly figure of Fahrenheit came hurrying toward us, waving his cane and surrounded by ten fanatics.

"Suze!" he called out. "Surely you cannot abdicate the antechambers of soft power to this monolabial!" — jabbing his stick toward me.

I replied that his linguistic legerdemain was too late, and that in any case the train was leaving.

"The tongue parchment rustles!" he cried with gusto. "When eyeing letters becomes the occupation of souls, you'll do better to publicize land ownership!"

I was scrabbling to formulate an appropriate response when I saw Koos rushing up with ten proselytes of his own, all bearing swagger sticks.

"There hang no cups but those that spill!" Koos rattled.

Fahrenheit stiffened. "Koos, Koos," he said paternally, "thunder crows from its outpost, making us mere lizards on the autobahn of inspiration."

"Rodents who skim off the top," snarled Koos, "are feed for the vultures of derision. We are all straw gods in the harsh light of our fingers."

Fahrenheit raised his cane with an offended bellow, and in an instant the quai was a flurry of sticks and recondite epithets, and the next thing I noticed was that the train had gone, and so had Suzanne.

※ ※ ※

Despite my best efforts, Suzanne's location resisted my searches. I stayed at home, unable to work, and took advantage of the cancellation of my lectures to pace the halls of my empty house. Claire had returned only to move out again, and I let myself fall prey to unshaven days and prolonged attempts at sleep. Every night I replayed on the dark but inventive ceiling of my room the perverse, oddly arousing scenes in which Suzanne co-starred with fat Fahrenheit. For the first time in my life I took up smoking (one, extract cigarette; two, strike match…). I saw no one, soon talked to no one, save for an unusually large portion of wrong numbers — but how I jumped at the phone every time! — and a couple of friends calling because they had heard (but how?) that "Claire and I were having difficulties": was there anything they could do? I deflected them as best I could.

Was this what life was like with and without Suzanne: everything haywire, sprung from its hinges? I passed through time in a state of acute malaise, all the while suspecting that I might never before have been so present in the world. And yet, there was so little I knew about her that after all my gnawing meditation I still wasn't sure where Suzanne ended and my fantasies took up. It began to seem that even the strange oppression I felt during her absences was created in my own image. These realizations, of course, had been applied to countless others by countless others before me. And of course, they alleviated nothing.

When finally we sat face-to-face, Suzanne recounted that Fahrenheit and his five remaining supporters had spent the week temporarily barricaded in an attic he'd rented, from where they launched and rebuffed attacks on and from Koos and his growing band of rebels. These attacks seemed to consist mainly in obscene phone calls made and received, but the result was that Fahrenheit and his dwindling back-up refused to leave the apartment for fear of a surprise assault. Suzanne had eventually slipped out — "I had enough of feeling like a gangster's moll when I was a kid," she said (referring to what, I wondered?) — and had spent a few days breathing the neutral air of the streets before pulling me from my own self-imposed exile.

We had a little time together, so little time together, before Fahrenheit's telegram reached in like the long arm of no law.

Since Fahrenheit's permanent apartment had been devastated — the last-minute frenzy of some wildcat renegades, even as Koos was calling off the war between himself and his ex-mentor — the poet had decided to remain in his rented attic barricade while workmen handled the restorations uptown. It was to these temporary lodgings that I went a few days after he'd sent word. Contrary to my expectations, I found no trace of the recent feud or of the café-table dictator; only a sad, somehow diminished Fahrenheit who opened the door to a narrow but fastidiously vacuumed garret.

"They're all gone," he said as we took our seats. "The last two snuck out the other day..." He reached over and plucked an apple from a bowl on the table, offered me one with eyebrow raised, then at my refusal went to the small sink and meticulously scrubbed the fruit. "Ablution is the solution to pollution," he confided. I felt my pocket for cigarettes.

Evidently furnished by the owner, the garret seemed ill-matched to Fahrenheit's physical and verbal expansiveness. The poet himself, as if trying to restore the balance of things, had visibly lost weight since our last encounter.

"I suppose you're wondering why I asked you here today," he said. "The simple fact is, my dear Schmidt, I've decided to put an end to these charades. Suze and I are to be married." My own eyebrows shot up in turn. "It's the best outcome for all concerned, don't you agree?..."

At a run, it took me half an hour to get from Fahrenheit's to Suzanne's.

Not long after returning from our brief seaside honeymoon, I came home from the university to find that Suzanne had disappeared. I made the usual inquiries, all the while knowing she'd return in due course. Lighting a cigarette, I sat at my desk to jot down some notes for the next day's lecture. One, two, one, two... When I read them back, they sounded like poetry.

Who Will Get Her?

~~~~~~~

"Who will get her?" Fieschi shouted out behind me, "which of us will it be?"

Ever since I first heard that phrase, practically in preschool, I've appreciated its musicality, but tonight at the Place de la Bastille it sent chills down my spine. Things seem clearer in summer than in winter: I was fed up with this clown. So I did my damnedest to get rid of him, to ditch him right then and there in the traffic in front of the half-built new opera house. Since we were kids everything has been up for grabs, be it marbles, a bike, a girl, or jacks, as though the world had been created to be divvied up between us. I usually sing my part rather loudly, but not tonight. I was speeding down the street like a maniac. "¡Olé!" yelled Fieschi, tightening his hold around my waist. I had a real soft spot for the jerk, but had he been run over by a truck before ten o'clock that would have suited me fine: that way I could have gone to the Perla and dined with Suzy alone. She had come into my life with the force of a fullfledged opera, while Fieschi snapped up any girl he liked with that "hands off" look of his. But Suzy was a woman, which changes everything: a real woman with circles under her eyes; a woman who was simply unhappy, something I had learned just that morning and that gave me a head start on him. My light tenor voice was coming back and melding with Fieschi's bass intonations, creating a rather good duo, if I do say so myself.

She had asked us to meet her at the Perla because she loved the place. It's because of the spinning wooden blades on the ceiling fans, she said, and the margaritas that make your head spin. After her third or fourth, her eyes became nearly as clear as Bellita's. She spoke about Mexico and Fieschi told her about the only book he ever managed to finish that is set there. But let's not get carried away: this would be the second time we were meeting at the Perla and I'd promised myself things wouldn't go the way they had the first time.

After that first night out with her, I had offered to take her wherever she liked: to the country, a park, the sea, the pool, the top of the Eiffel Tower, even, but she wasn't interested, in anything. I would have given her the world, and behind my back Fieschi would have done the same. But Suzy, in a very nice way, using her very nice voice, said no, tomorrow perhaps and then the next day it would be no again. Over the phone her voice put me into a real sweat. It sounded like she had just been woken by the phone's ring and that you had slipped right under the sheets with her. It was hot enough, but the very idea of a woman like that sleeping her way through the summer drove me crazy. It would be more understandable in winter. I tried to imagine someone in bed with her, but if there had been, she wouldn't have sounded so languid, wouldn't have been stayed on the phone so long. No, I had a gut feeling that she didn't have anyone and my instincts never fail, or else it was

Who Will Get Her?

someone far away, whereas for the moment I was living right next door — twenty-five miles is only a half an hour away on a motorcycle.

"What could a woman of the world see in a guy who's not even thirty years old yet?" I asked Bellita. Bellita has answered every one of my questions since I was born.

"No, it's not that. No, no, child, it's got nothing to do with age. Maybe the woman you're talking about is simply unhappy." I must admit that it will be hard for me to grow up as long as Bellita continues to call me "child," but the way she says it, it's endearing, even a compliment. To her there are men and there are children, and the best thing one can do to avoid being the worst kind of male (my father) is to belong to the race of children. So I reformulated my question: What can a child do about a woman being simply unhappy? Bellita pulled a cigarette from the platinum case — the color of her hair — that I had given her for her sixtieth birthday and she thought long and hard as she smoked, unlike Suzy who is always in a rush to put out her Rich & Lights just to light up another. Then she gave me an answer: "Don't hate the part of her that makes her unhappy. Don't try to strip her of her unhappiness." Remarkable, don't you think? I'm not saying this because Bellita's my mother, but she *is* a genius.

So when Fieschi left the table to go chat up the waitress or take a piss, or whatever, I worked up as much courage as I possibly could. I needed it that memorable night at the Perla, because Suzy was already naked. Completely naked underneath the flowered print dress, the way women are in summer.

Girls find a way to be just a bit naked all the time, even when it's snowing; but Suzy Schmidt was a woman from top to bottom. The bun of her hair was held in place by a single pin. For the past two hours it had seemed on the point of falling, just like her dress, and yet it didn't. Right, so I put my hand on her naked shoulder, slipped a finger beneath the little silk strap and let her have it in one breath: "I care for you very much, Suzy, and I'd love you less if you weren't so unhappy."

She gave me one of those looks whose meaning is clear as day. I don't know whether it was my hand or my words that managed to get through to her but she was touched. I had established a link between us, a fragile silken link, a tiny bridge of sorts, which although unseen was there all the same! The air began to hum with the same intensity it gets when two people are about to kiss for the first time. Naturally that was precisely the moment that stupid Fieschi chose to come back on the scene, from behind as usual. He bent over us, right smack between our faces like a moth caught in a spiderweb and in the smoothest bass tones, he whispered: "Which will it be, Suzy, which of us will get you in the end?"

I don't know whether laughter is a symptom of women's unhappiness, but from that moment on Suzy didn't stop laughing. "Let's drink this Margarita under the table!" Fieschi shouted with that keen humor of his. And it started all over again, just like the first time. The three of us got drunk, jumped on my Norton, drove the wrong way down one-way streets, and just barely missed getting nabbed by the cops. The only difference being that at the door of the building where we dropped her off, he had an idea: "What are we doing tomorrow, since it's Sunday?"

"Let's go have lunch in Meaux," I said, taking my turn at improvisation.

"Bellissimo-oh-oh," raved my friend, who had a passion for Bellita. "I'll take the train with Suze."

"The train?" Suzy said, speaking up. "Why can't we drive?"

That was when I struck from behind myself, saying: "He hasn't got a car anymore, he wrecked it, so he can go alone on the train and I'll come by on my bike about noon to pick you up, o.k.? Get on, Fieschi, I'm taking you home!" That was how I cut short the good-byes, which are hopeless when there are three of you.

At noon she sounded like she was still asleep over the intercom, despite the ringing of the bells. She had taken some sleeping pills the night before and wasn't dressed yet. I jumped at the chance to go wait for her upstairs, but she preferred to meet me in front. Doors don't need to swing wide for Suzy, she would fit through the eye of a needle. Dressed in a loose chemise, tight-fitting trousers, and her ballet pumps that day, she stepped as softly onto the blacktop as if she were getting out of bed. I didn't hear her coming. My hands trembled as I handed her the helmet I had given Bellita as a thank-you for my Norton. "Who's Bellita?" she finally asked after fifteen minutes on the highway. I answered using Fieschi's expression: "The most beautiful eyes in the body." Usually that gets a reaction, but it had no effect on her. "THE MOST BEAUTIFUL EYES IN THE BODY," I shouted several decibels louder.

S. ~~~~~~~~~~~

Oh well, I wouldn't have to unravel the enigma: she was sound asleep at ninety miles an hour! Then, for no apparent reason, she awoke. Was it the episcopal palace my mother lives in as curator of the museum located just below? Was it the little bouquet of garden roses on the table that she smelled? Was it the bream ready for the oven on its bed of lemon, tomato, and onion slices? All of a sudden she liked it all, and she was both hungry and thirsty. She repeated the phrase, *The most beautiful eyes in the body,* when I introduced them.

"When will that boy ever give up hounding me with that nickname, at my age and about to retire!" Bellita exclaimed. Pauline and Fieschi both protested in my favor. I have no idea what kind of stories he'd told about our Saturday night out, but as I uncorked the second bottle Bellita made a graceful swaying gesture with her hand for my benefit.

Aside from that, there wasn't a single cloud over the day nor over Suzy's expression, except maybe when Pauline turned to her with finger pensively pointed to her forehead and said, "Your name reminds me of a Schmidt I once knew at the college in Orlando. If I remember right, he was…" Our American friend is an obsessive cross-referencer. For her, a name must always remind her of someone and a noun of something. Bellita claims that this quirk is worse than a simple flaw: it shows a lack of respect for the present.

That's when Fieschi gave me a wink. He clanged his little spoon against the water pitcher, smiling like Dracula, and interrupted this bit of nostalgia with: "And how about my name, Pauline, doesn't it remind you of an assassination?"

~~~~~~~~ *Who Will Get Her?*

And yet, my mother's friend isn't all that bad. She teaches at Central Florida University in the winter, and in summers she goes to Europe to isolate herself and study. In museums and libraries, preferably in Italy where Bellita goes to meet her, or this year at the Louvre and the Bibliothèque Nationale. Thanks to which I had gone to spend my month of vacation with them in Meaux and met Suzy in Paris one night, in the Pacifico. She was having dinner alone; I wasn't, and needless to say, without Fieschi I would never have gotten up the nerve to speak to that very naked woman who was clearly setting the men of August on fire.

Now, according to Fieschi, we had a chance with Suzy for the very reason that she was tired of men. Inasmuch as we were "children," that is. She knew all about men and books, but apparently little about music or painting, not to mention angels' wings! Since Pauline had not been able to resist telling her all about her thesis, which was inspired by one of Bellita's studies called "Angels' Wings in Pre-Renaissance Painting," Suzy was mesmerized. She must not have seen too many in her life. Bellita started off by pulling out my favorite for her, Fra Angelico. After a half-hour of going through her collection, Fieschi and I were already bored, but she saw fit to mention that there were two more just one floor below us.

While Bellita gave a guided tour of the museum we knew by heart, Fieschi and I stayed behind to flirt with Pauline. As soon as Bellita turns her back it becomes our favorite sport. Poor Pauline is petrified just like the first day, as if she hasn't yet understood that *we* understand, that we're simply having a

S. ~~~~~~~~~~~~

good time putting her on and that the whole thing is funnier that way.

After the tour, Suzy nestled in the sagging armchair, her head tilted back like someone in the first row of a cinema, and watched every move Bellita made. As though she had never seen anyone make tea in her life. Fieschi claimed he had to leave, supposedly to work: he had to hand in the musical score for a film that had been commissioned by the composer himself — one of those guys who don't write anymore, but who still put their names to the scores for money. I would have been more than happy to make another trip to Paris and back if Suzy hadn't preferred this time to take the train with Fieschi. I must have looked a bit uneasy, because she whispered in my ear, keeping her eyes on Bellita all the while: "She tells me that you're leaving at the end of the week. Be sure to call me — we don't have much time…" After hearing that, I could walk them both to the train station without a worry on my mind. I was soaring.

No way to get hold of Fieschi on Monday. I wanted him to tell me about the trip back. Impossible to find him, either at his ex-wife's house where the piano still was, or at the studio. That evening he finally deigned to call me, but I had already been reassured: Suzy had made a date with me for two o'clock the next afternoon. He, on the other hand, sounded depressed. He had spent the day with his benefactor. Tough day. I sympathised, then tried to direct his thoughts back to yesterday; but he was no more interested in yesterday than in tomorrow. The only thing he could find to say about my date was that it was "understandable"! "That's understandable," he said, "considering you're Bellita's son. Ms. Schmidt has never known anyone as soothing, never seen anyone as beautiful, or as serene, and so on and so forth. Apparently you even look like her in some ways, not in the eyes or the soul, but lower down, in the mouth. Really amazing!"

I myself didn't find it all that surprising that Suzy should react to Bellita the way everyone else does. To give him a laugh, I told him the one thing that Pauline had finally come up with, a real killer: "Personally, I don't like brunettes."

"That's understandable," Fieschi said, "Suzy doesn't like Pauline either." I didn't press it. When he's ghost writing, Fieschi thinks that everything, including indentured servitude, is understandable.

Now Suzy was burning with an ardent desire to meet archangels and seraphim. She didn't know that she had all Eternity to do so. That's when I came up with the unfortunate idea of going to the Louvre — she loved it, but we met with closed doors. I'll never understand why I had to choose the weekly closing day to visit a public museum, and my gaffe was made doubly ridiculous by the fact that it came from a curator's son. We wandered through the construction site, where they had just started building the new entrance. Luckily the Palais-Royal gardens weren't far off.

When she slipped her arm around my neck to pull me closer, I thought she meant to forgive me for the Louvre being closed. Not at all, she wanted to kiss me, which she did with a rather uncommon determination. She kissed me on the mouth, in front of the fountain and the mothers with underage children. She, who had never so much as touched me before, kissed me right there in public, and so naturally that I was left dumbfounded. It was the kind of torrid kiss that would have aroused me anywhere else but in that park; the night before I would have lent my Norton for a kiss like that. But at that moment, either out of surprise or nervousness, I didn't even feel happy about it. Besides, daytime kisses don't have as much of a future as nighttime kisses. I prefer nighttime, and choosing the moment myself. All the same, I held her tightly against me as we walked, my hand on her rising and falling hip, and began to realize how happy I truly was, began to fly sky high. But just as I was preparing to enter heaven's gate, she refused to let me take her home. She had an important appointment — for her work, she made sure to say. The word sounded odd coming out of her mouth. I didn't even catch a glimpse of her as she disappeared into a taxi. From the lowered window she cried, "Call me tomorrow!" Since our kiss she had been using a more intimate tone with me.

The next day, as if she had planned it, she proposed that we have dinner together at the Perla or the Pacifico, *without* Fieschi. Well, strange as it might seem, I didn't hesitate — I'll say it again, I did *not* hesitate — but willingly explained to her that I wasn't free that evening, that I'd promised to spend it with Bellita. She and Pauline wanted to go see an old Antonioni film that was being shown in the Latin Quarter, one that starred *one of our favorite actrices*, they had both made a point of saying to convince me. To see Lucia Bose they would be ready to subject me to the worst kind of torture! Afterward, I was to treat them to dinner at the Coupole. All of this had the atmosphere of a night out just for the three of us, no doubt the last one we would have before I headed back to my little part of the country, before I went back to organizing musical exchanges between Montpellier, Toulouse, and Barcelona — my life as a provincial traveling salesman, sneered the anti-provincial Fieschi.

"Oh, could I join you?" she blurted out. Why hadn't I thought of it myself? It was the perfect solution. Even the slight doubts I had entertained in Meaux couldn't erase this certainty.

"Then invite Fieschi along as well!" Bellita exclaimed, oddly. "Since we're no longer a threesome, we might as well make it a fivesome."

Fair enough — and I no more wanted to contradict her than I wanted to spend the evening alone with three women. *He* was the one who made a fuss: "So what is it you want from me, old man? To go see *Just Women* by that incredible bore Antonioni, sitting between Pauline and Bellita while you act the lovebird with Ms. Schmidt? Or should I go on playing *The Chandelier* by the unforgettable Alfred, between Ms. Schmidt and you?" I hate it when Fieschi refers to Suzy that way — it makes her sound older — but I kept my annoyance hidden.

I tried to take a sentimental tack: "Never mind all that, come on, I'm leaving on Saturday. After that, you can have her all to yourself," I even had the hypocritical audacity to add.

So it was that after the film (one of those depressing movies where everything falls apart between the characters) the five of us ended up at the Coupole, Fieschi and I rather morose as we listened to the women's comments. It's amazing how much women find to say about things like movies. Personally, I didn't feel the need to make any of my opinions known, and then Pauline told us she was thinking of going to Barcelona. Suddenly life was sweet again. I was supposed to accompany an Occitan choir that was going to perform there at the Liceu at the beginning of September, and Pauline was asking Bellita whether she wanted to go there at the same time, just before she headed back to Florida for the winter. Despite her efforts to explain her theory of Catalan angels, with all those wings to find, it was clear that she was simply proposing the trip to please Bellita — and, by extension, me. I didn't get a chance to thank her, but such pleasant surprises come in bunches, and the next thing I heard was Suzy exclaiming: "What a marvelous coincidence! I have to go to Barcelona at the same time — for that job I told you about," she said, turning to me.

I couldn't believe my ears. I was still imagining myself walking down the Ramblas between the two women of my life, while the others were rushing to change the conversation. It all went too fast. Because that idiot Fieschi had spotted a tatoo of a blue anchor on the forearm of someone sitting at a nearby table, we went from talking about wings to symbols, spots, and assorted permanent marks. Bellita, who deserved her name more than ever that night, laughingly revealed that we both had the same birthmark, and that on the day of Resurrection we would have less trouble finding each other than everyone else thanks to our distinctive sign. Was Suzy listening? With a lost, faraway look, even worse than Lucia Bose's in the film, she whispered that she didn't feel well and preferred to go home so as not to ruin our night out. I could see it would have been useless to try to keep her there. I walked her out to the taxi. I was terribly concerned about leaving her alone in such a state. "You're wrong about that," said Pauline, who clearly had something against her. "She just thinks it'll make her interesting."

"She *is* interesting," I replied.

Fieschi didn't say a word, as he was intently contemplating the empty table next to us, which had been abandoned by its diners. It was late and people were going home. "We should be going, too," Bellita concluded. The night had not turned out well.

That woman certainly was a thorny rose; she left you feeling all torn up inside. On Thursday I felt the sting: she had reverted to her old self and no longer wanted to see me, no longer wanted anything, except the date of the concert at the Liceu. And then on Friday, the night before I was to leave, her mood changed once more and she asked me to go for a walk in the fresh air. The very idea of fresh air tires me straight off, unless it's sea air. Unfortunately, we didn't have time to go to the seashore, and besides she had a forest in mind.

Usually I take the lead, but that afternoon I felt like a kid being lead around by his nose. It was she who decided what direction to take, which exit, the highway, the trail, the path right down to the tree we stretched out under in the

Fontainebleau forest. She ran her fingers over my body as though the woods were her bedroom. She opened my shirt, undid the buttons one by one and then my beltbuckle as well. With wide-open eyes she examined my shoulders, my chest, my stomach. My hands found shelter under her dress between her bare legs, but she wouldn't let me have a look to be sure this was really happening. She went on undressing me and I suddenly felt her tongue on my skin, licking at the small birthmark on my left hip, while with her hand she made me come, too fast, like a child. The sun had begun to penetrate the forest; we were now in daylight, and a bit of saliva glistened around the small birthmark on my hip.

Even this time, which would be our last since I was leaving at daybreak, she wouldn't let me come up to her apartment. And like a poor fool, as I stood there at the front door to her building, I began to count the hours until I could see her again.

Bellita took me in her arms. At least *her* eyes didn't avoid mine. "Don't leave so early, child," she advised. "Don't make the whole trip in one day, it's too tiring. Leave after breakfast and stop somewhere on the way. You'll still have all of Sunday to get to Toulouse. Otherwise I'll worry too much." I let her convince me without much resistance. I was exhausted. Disappointments are exhausting. I think that I would have been able to sleep straight through to the beginning of September had I not been awakened by something out of the ordinary in Meaux. The sound of an argument or tears. Bellita had raised her voice, which never happens. It was out of the question to go to Barcelona under these conditions. What conditions? I listened silently behind the door, but poor Pauline wasn't helping any. Her sobs were hacking the truth into bits: "That perverse brunette... all brunettes... understood immediately... what a *bitch*... on the day he was leaving... as though I didn't even exist... and he, *and he*..." It was definitely about me, because I clearly and distinctly heard my mother say that no one had the right to call her son blind. "Blinded, I'll admit. But as far as *I'm* concerned, she won't get anywhere." That's when I lost it and opened the door.

Pauline was sitting there in the sagging armchair, in tears, with one of my handkerchiefs in her hand. Bellita was leaning over and consoling her. On the floor was a huge bouquet of flowers still in its cellophane wrapping. Also on the floor was an envelope addressed to my mother and a calling card that I picked up:

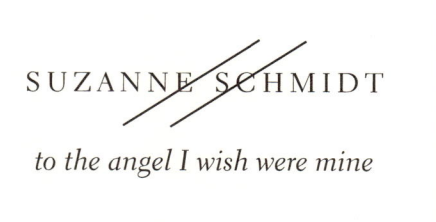

SUZANNE SCHMIDT

to the angel I wish were mine

At around noon I called Fieschi to say goodbye. No comment. I think he'd already understood. All I could do was confirm it: neither of us would get her.

— *translated by Matthew Escobar*

Let Us Pray

"He's dying, I tell you." "I can't come," Susan had the cheek to say.

"But this heart attack has done him in. He hasn't got much longer."

"It's impossible."

"He's been asking for you and you're the only one I can turn to. I've been running myself into the ground trying to care for your father and manage the bar. What kind of woman *are* you, anyway?"

She hesitated, then whispered into the receiver, "Well, maybe for a little while..."

"A little while is all he has!" I said before slamming down the phone.

In the fifteen years Fotopolis and I had been married, he rarely talked about his daughter. Once I found some old photographs in a drawer in the back room. She was just a teenager, but I could tell it was Susan, looking like a little tart with mascara so thick she might have applied it with a paint brush. A couple of hoodlums in black leather jackets were hanging all over her.

I'd first met her when she was married to her third hus-

S. ~~~~~~~~~~~

band, a college teacher named Schmidt. He stared at Fotopolis and me like we were a couple of bushmen and asked a lot of stupid questions. Meanwhile Susan paced the flat like a caged tiger and stared wild-eyed at the sea. Altogether it was an unpleasant visit; I thought she acted like a bitch.

To look at us you wouldn't guess we were nearly the same age. Susan had a tiny figure and kept her long dark hair straight. She was one of those women who look young from behind and surprise you when they turn around wearing an older face—except even her face was still young, with those eyes of hers all blue and expressive. They gave her an innocent, almost spiritual look.

It's been different for me. The sun hasn't been kind to my freckled skin. My red hair's faded, shot with grey. As for my figure, I lost it years ago; living with Fotopolis meant eating with Fotopolis, and Fotopolis lived to eat. When the old man gave up gambling he turned to food, but he was already no toreador when we met.

It seems an eternity since I came to Ostend for a week's holiday with my sister Clarice. Neither of us was tied down. She was celebrating her divorce, and though I had a gentleman friend in Greenwich, he was married. Clarice and I spent our days on the beach sunning and swimming in the sea and our nights drinking at the Blue Anchor.

Fotopolis was the bartender. We talked and joked with him into the night and he entertained us with his bungled card tricks. One evening Clarice went back early to our hotel because of sunburn. I had a touch of it myself, but stayed on in the Blue Anchor until closing. Fotopolis asked me to his rooms above the bar. He wasn't much to look at, but he wasn't married, either.

I love living here by the sea. I like walking the promenade and watching all the life. It suits me.

"Look who's here!" I called to Fotopolis as I led Susan into the flat. She arrived by train that next afternoon wearing a grey Paris suit and a red felt hat with a brim that shadowed her face. Black kid gloves grazed her wrists.

"Hello, Father." Her voice was low and sad as she touched his shoulder with the leather tips of her fingers.

Fotopolis lay on a cot set up in the front room by a window overlooking the port. Covered with only a sheet, he looked for all the world like an overstuffed sofa put up for the summer. For him to roll over was an undertaking that left him unable to speak; but his eyes, sunken beneath yellowish purple bags, lit up at the sight of his only child.

I showed Susan to the spare room at the back of the flat.

"I know the way, Paula," she said pushing past me, dragging her suitcase and acting like she was angry. "I lived in this room when I was a girl."

I tried to be pleasant. "It must bring back a lot of memories."

"Yes." Susan creaked the springs of the mattress. "It does."

Waiting with Fotopolis while she unpacked, I noticed that he smelled of urine and his hair was greasy. His arms were a mass of bruises from all the needles. Someone needs to put

S. ~~~~~~~~~~~~

him out of his misery, I thought, remembering how Clarice warned against marriage with an older man. The first ten years had been okay. Then, all at once, he caved in.

I was surprised to see Susan come out of her room wearing a simple cotton shift. "He needs a bath," she said with a sniff.

"It ain't been easy," I shot back. "Takes two just to roll him over."

That night, Susan sat with Fotopolis while I went downstairs and looked after business. When we were first married, Fotopolis had gambling debts against the bar. I put a stop to that! Now the Blue Anchor was in ship shape and there was a good sum in the bank. The less said about money to Susan, the better. After all, wasn't it me that did all the work and looked after the old man besides?

Lately I let the word out that I was looking for a manager. We'd never had one before; it had always been just Fotopolis and me running things. But with him sick, I had no choice.

There aren't many people you can trust, yet the moment Willie walked in the bar I could tell there was something special about him. He was an American seaman and said he was part Cherokee Indian, but I guessed he had a lot more Negro in him than anything else. With tattoos of serpents and spider webs and other disgusting creatures from his wrists up to his shoulders, he looked quite savage enough. His long arms were corded with muscles from hard work at sea, but the rest of him was tight and smooth with skin the color of curry.

"Where are you from in America?" I asked, serving him a whiskey.

"Baton Rouge. But I ship out of Galveston." He downed his shot.

"Why aren't you looking for work on a boat?"

"I need someplace to cool out," he answered, averting his dark eyes.

I had no earthly idea what he was talking about and surprised myself when I offered him his chance at the Blue Anchor. Willie gave a sudden, wide smile, showing me his very white but broken teeth.

"You'll have to wear a shirt with long sleeves," I warned. I liked him but there was something indecent about those arms.

Now that I had help, I could spend a few minutes here or there sitting with Fotopolis to relieve Susan. It was at those times I pulled out my old Bible, for it's only fitting that a dying man make peace with his Creator. The way I was brought up, I never thought reading the Good Book could do you any harm, but if you had seen how it made Susan carry on, you'd think she was possessed. She never said anything but, from the moment I began, she put on the most disapproving scowl and started crashing around the flat tidying up. It was impossible to heard over such a racket.

Finally I said to her, "I may not be an educated woman, not an intellectual like you, but I know better than to mock the word of God." From then on, whenever I picked up my Bible, she headed for her room or out the door.

She was a miserable creature but she had a healthful effect

on Fotopolis. After his heart attack, I didn't think he would last the week. But when Susan came, the old man seemed to improve. His color was better and he slept through the night. She massaged him. She exercised his limbs. I don't know how she managed to hoist those hams: I sure didn't have the patience for it. She even took to reading her books to him, until he let her know with faint groans that he preferred the Bible to most of what she brought with her.

And so she began reading scripture: page after page for hours on end. I started getting tired of it myself. A verse here, a chapter there, that's all well and good. But Susan began with *Genesis* and all the begats. Soon she was up to Moses and the Israelites. Now I've never minded the Psalms; they're restful. But the books of the prophets! I got sick to death with the troubles of Job. Soon I was sneaking down to the Blue Anchor to drink shots with Willie.

Well, one day I was coming up from the bar and found Susan sitting at her father's side with the Bible open in her lap. She was pale as a ghost and tears were streaming down her cheeks.

"What!" I screamed. "Is he dead?" I rushed to the bed but the old man was only snoring.

"No, Paula," she said quietly, "it's not Father; it's me. My life has been such a waste, so empty. God is punishing me!"

"You've been reading too much Bible," I told her straight out.

"And it's you I have to thank." She rose to her feet, holding her hands out to me.

Involuntarily I drew back. I thought she had gone off the deep end at last. "Go on. I was just doing my duty."

But Susan, as if struck with an inspiration, sank to her knees and cried, "I beg you, Paula, teach me how to pray!" Her blue eyes were large and pleading. She caught my hands and pulled me down. She wouldn't have it any other way but that I should get on my knees. Me! With my arthritis!

I put her through the Lord's Prayer. She drank in the words. Then we moved on to the Apostle's Creed. She mumbled each phrase after mine. "Yes," she said, "yes, I believe. Is there more?"

"Well," I said, trying to shift my weight a little, "one usually makes a prayer of confession."

"A prayer of confession?"

"You must list all your sins, the ones you truly repent. You ask God to forgive them. You ask Him to cleanse you of your vices—careful there."

"Yes, I understand." She brushed her hair back from her face.

"Now you don't have to make your confession out loud. It's between you and the Lord." I started to rise. "I'll just hop back down to the bar..."

Susan's hand gripped my shoulder like a vice, holding me in place. "No, Paula. Please stay. You must pray for me."

So I tried to make a prayer for her but my knees were killing me! Every time I thought she was about to finish, she would sigh deeply, wrinkle her brow and begin again.

It was already going on half an hour when, all at once, a

great groan rose from the sleeping man. Susan leapt up; it took me a moment longer on account of my knees. Fotopolis was gasping for air and spittle foamed from his mouth. His eyes rolled back in his head and he started to shake, a human earthquake as his heart exploded. In the arms of his wife and daughter, Fotopolis slipped from this life.

"Praise God!" Susan cried. "The Lord's hand is at work in my life." She was holding the senseless head of Fotopolis to her breast.

"What are you talking about?" I was stunned. "He's dead!"

"Father's life hung by a thread until my moment of revelation and repentance. With his death, I'm born again in faith. It's a miracle!"

That was Susan for you. Here is her poor old father, dead as a doornail, and all she can think of is herself. She dropped Fotopolis' head on the pillow and, picking up my Bible, hustled back to her room looking feverish and muttering some nonsense about three days of "prayer and fasting."

"Three days of prayer and fasting ain't going to bring back your father!" I yelled after her, but she didn't hear.

I sat a few minutes at the side of my dead husband trying to think what to feel. Him lying there so stony still, it gave me the shivers. I didn't want to be alone and Susan was no help, so I went back down to the Blue Anchor to give Willie the news.

We discussed funeral arrangements and it was Willie who suggested a burial at sea. What was the point of calling in an undertaker? Why waste money on a coffin? And funeral wreathes are depressing. There were no throngs to mourn him: just Susan and me. It was a brilliant idea. We all knew Fotopolis loved the sea. But how could we do it?

"My man Crowbar's got a boat," Willie said. He smiled and refilled my glass with brandy. "Just give me the word."

"Does tonight seem too soon?" I sounded a bit anxious, and I was. I didn't want to wait for Fotopolis to start smelling up the flat. And I knew I wouldn't sleep easy with a dead man lying about.

"Get it over with," Willie encouraged me. "I'll give Crowbar a shout right now."

I patted down my hair, finally realizing how frightful I must have looked after my ordeal. It was so good to have someone to lean on.

I went back to the flat to tell Susan, afraid she might not approve of our plan and insist on a church funeral. She opened her door a crack while I tried to explain how expensive the doctors had been.

"As you wish." Her face was in the shadow of the door; her voice was a harsh whisper. "I will be ready."

Willie closed the bar early; it had been a slow night anyway. He came up the stairs to ask if I needed help. Letting him in, he looked around. "Nice place you got here."

We dressed Fotopolis in his only suit. Willie tied his tie and I combed his hair and parted it in the middle the way Fotopolis liked. I put a pair of dice and a deck of cards in his pocket just for luck; maybe things would be different for him up there.

S. ~~~~~~~~~~~

"He looks great," Willie told me.

At midnight Crowbar came around with the car. It took three of us to carry the body down the stairs, then Fotopolis almost got stuck as we tried to push him into the back seat. In all the commotion, I almost forgot about Susan. Crowbar was smitten when she emerged from the side entrance with her face shrouded in a black lace mantilla. Willie and Crowbar sat up front. Fotopolis was propped up in the back seat, between Susan and me. I jumped when his head rolled on my shoulder.

On board the launch, Crowbar provided ropes and concrete blocks. As we motored out the channel, Willie worked on fixing these to the body. I didn't care to look. The seas were high but we went beyond the second bar. Susan began raving some nonsense about the sea and death visited twice. "Mesmaeker!" she whispered.

"Lady, if you think you can do a cleaner job, be my guest," snapped Willie. He didn't have any patience with Susan.

When Willie finished tying the knots, I laid my hand across Fotopolis' womanish breast. "Good-by, old boy," I murmured. "You were a good husband but no catch."

Willie and his friend hoisted the body over the side. It was a beautiful moment, with the moon coming out from behind the clouds and shining across the black waves. Susan watched the body sink and recited a a few appropriate verses.

On the way back to the Blue Anchor, she rode in front with Crowbar, and Willie and I were in the back. Willie held my hand consolingly. Crowbar remained fascinated with Susan even when she started grilling him on points of theology; but as soon as he stopped the engine, Susan tripped out the door and disappeared up the stairs. I gave Willie the money to split with Crowbar who, miffed at Susan's departure, declined to share a post-funeral drink in the bar.

"I guess the Blue Anchor is all yours now," said Willie, raising his glass.

"Yes, but it won't be the same without..." I started to go on like a proper widow when Willie gently put his hand across my lips.

"Baby, you may never miss him." He pinched my cheek and gave me a devilish wink.

"You're a naughty one!" I screeched. It seemed like the first good laugh I'd had in years.

Susan kept her promise to fast and pray for three days. How she lived I don't know. When she finally crept out of her hole, she looked weak but resolute. "I'm ready to begin my penance," she said coming into the bar. "Put me to work."

Willie and I looked at one another. You don't want a crazy creature like that hanging around a respectable bar. It's bad for business and makes the customers uncomfortable with all that scripture quoting. Besides, Susan was like the ghost of Fotopolis, casting a pall over my hopes and dreams. I knew it was a little soon and that Willie was so much younger, but how many more chances would I have?

"My dear," I said to her, "this is no place to begin the practice of a Christian life. There are too many temptations. Go up to the church and talk to Father Breton. He's very kind. He'll know more about handling conversions than we do."

That was about the worst advice I have ever given. Susan, dressed in sack cloth and ashes, took herself up to church. Every day she went to mass and spent the balance of the mornings mooning about the confessionals. She bought decks of holy cards and ropes of rosaries. She nearly set the church ablaze lighting candles before the shrines. When she started bringing candles home, Willie told me, "She's got to go."

I visited old Father Breton, who agreed she might need some guidance. Two days later Susan came into the bar, eyes shining. "Paula, a way has been opened to me."

"You don't say." I was drying glasses. Father Breton had heard of a religious leader very far away who ministered to a colony of laity devoted to the ideal of renunciation. Isolated and contemplative, their ways were simple and their diet meager. "Sounds perfect," I said. "Should do you a world of good."

"Pray for me, Paula, that I may be found worthy."

I prayed.

Willie and I saw Susan to the railroad station where she took the train to Calais; our farewells were simple but heartfelt. The same afternoon, Willie moved his things up to the flat. That night after we closed the Blue Anchor, I lay wrapped in the jungle of his arms and he told me about his tattooed beasts. The bull, he said, was for strength. The serpent was for cunning. "And what about all those spider webs?" I asked.

"Those," he said, "are to hold you."

A regular Eden, it was.

The Quevedo Cipher
~~~~~~

I laid out my tools on THE HOTEL BEDSPREAD: FIVE lengths of cord, a leather gag, mushroom powders.

Comfortable, anonymous, safe, La Perla satisfied my needs. At the front desk I had experienced some anxiety when the receptionist, an elderly Levantine, glanced up from my passport and said, "I believe I knew you elsewhere, although not as a Triestine." For a matter of seconds I forgot my current name, and stammer points began glowing in my nape. (I shall not censor my stutter. That would make it worse.) Before I had to respond, he began leading the way to my room.

On the bed, parallel to the "tools," I placed my card — Karl-Ignaz Molinaro, Direttore Commerciale, Assicurazioni Lloyd Triestino — and the report sheets on my three women: Paula Fotopolis, Claire McDonald, Madame Lothar Schmidt. The names had once belonged to S, born Fotopolis, her first husband a McDonald, her third a Schmidt. The women had all three been born in Belgium sixty-two years before. Beneath each name an address and telephone number had been typed, as well as another name to use when I introduced myself.

If none of these women proved to be S, my months-long quest would come to a forlorn end. My correspondents had investigated every city and village on this Mediterranean Sea

S. ~~~~~~~~~~~~

to whose shores I knew she had come. That was all I knew of her. I had toured those shores. My search would end in this town.

I dined at Fahrenheit 451, at the receptionist's recommendation. His earlier remark set me musing, after I had begun my dinner, on the many other names I had previously used in my career: Mr. Haak in Croatia, in Mesopotamia Henry Shah... They had abetted my progress to prosperity. Whatever happened now, Karl-Ignaz would be my last disguise.

While I ate, I resumed reading my golfing farce, *Par Seven*, and finished it with the cheese. Its climax described an exceptional chip shot that dropped straight into the seventh hole, whose cup was mysteriously connected to a septic tank beneath it; an off-color geyser resulted. (Much as I love angel wings, I refused dessert.) The player, who with this shot became the first ever to make par on the hole, earned the right to baptize it with the female name of his choice.

I needed something else to read. For the past thirty-seven years no day of my life has been spent without a book at hand. I therefore paid my first visit to one of the town's landmarks, a bar called L'Iris de Souss. Underneath the name, its sign read:

> Spécialité de gentianes
> Book Bar
> Anna Delaforge, Prop.

On the shelves behind the counter, against a wall-length

mirror, bright bottles alternated with darker books — a comforting sight, spoiled only by the brief pang I felt when from the door I spied the tiny, well-proportioned figure of the owner, almost a replica of S's. A flurry of hope was erased as soon as I noticed her blue-tinged, frilly hair, her brown eyes, the flat cross of white gold nestled between her breasts. I nevertheless welcomed the sight of Anna Delaforge as a favorable omen. After inviting her to join me in a drink, I took out a book and retired to La Perla.

The Quevedo Cipher bored me, no doubt because I at once solved the cipher of the title. Its first demonstration, a passage entitled "An Englishman Heads East," made its secret all too obvious:

> By hazard nabbed in Mecca, he was befuddled, wretched, and miffed. He was ragged, then withheld (by rigid raj-jarring) from trekking on. A sullen backgammoner, he was stunned by rococo poppers from an Iraq-queered, weak-starred, misshapen steam fitter. At sunup he revved his new-wound fax-xerox-telex and, without as much as a by-your-leave, buzzed away.

I stopped reading and distracted myself until sleep by using the cipher to encrypt my fancies. One example only, one only:

> Miss Hammer's full of essential latter-day pessimism. Without trust, she muffles my efforts to see her marred.

* * *

S. ~~~~~~~~~~~

Next morning I called at the records office in the town hall. I wanted to verify my information about the three women and, if possible, to obtain more. The clerk I was directed to proved skeptical at the outset, subsequently mistrustful, and finally, when I tendered a lunch-size bank note, indignant. Pursing his lips, letting his arms fall to his sides, with a flick of his eyebrows he set me on my way to the door.

After telephoning Paula Fotopolis, I drove my rented fan car to her address outside of town: a broad three-story house surrounded by a walled park. As I approached the gate, a young zebra stared out at me through its high bars.

A gardener let me in. Mrs. Fotopolis, who was neither Belgian, nor small, nor blue-eyed, answered my initial question by explaining that, two months previously, mounting expenses had forced the municipal zoo to close down. Its animals were first auctioned off. Despite considerable publicity, the sale was not a success. She herself had bought the zebra, a few others had bid for ponies or peacocks; most beasts found no takers. Even the exquisite Mesmaeker fauns, who when the dealer approached them had remained perfectly still, with heads bowed and forelegs crossed, were in the end eaten by the auctioneers.

Our conversation was interrupted by a telephone call. I overheard Mrs. Fotopolis say, "I'll look after Bodley Head, you invite Cape, she can handle the other." On her return she informed me that she was organizing a convention, scheduled to coincide with the town's annual fiesta, of a random sampling of American and British publishers.

The Quevedo Cipher

"We're trying to anticipate every difficulty after the disaster of last year's fiesta — first disease in the vineyards, then the dust hashish riots. Our celebration is not meant to be an orgiastic spree."

I learned several facts about the fiesta. It begins at the ninth new moon after the vernal equinox. It lasts three days. Predictable processions frame less formal gatherings, all supervised by specially marked police, haughty in manner but more helpful than severe. Music of great antiquity is played during concerts conducted from atop traditionally sculpted farm wagons. In many a square and park the oldest of the region's dances is performed. On the second evening a chapel dedicated to Saint Novellus is opened for vespers, which is the only service celebrated there in the course of the church year; a priest is specially sent from Rome to officiate. A statement whose opening words are spoken by the mayor to inaugurate the fiesta is continued by his deputy and then for seventy-two hours passed from one citizen to another without ever being allowed a pause longer than the equivalent of a comma; each human link of this verbal chain must not stop speaking, whatever the hour or circumstances, until a willing successor has been found. (I was grateful for this information when accosted one night by a babbling local.)

Mrs. Fotopolis inquired after the supposed acquaintance whose name I had mentioned when I called her. I had anticipated the question. I replied that I had come with the hope that she could supply this very news.

I eventually attended the vespers service at Saint Novellus's.

S. ~~~~~~~~~~~

I did so in order to study the remains of the frescoes Chardin had painted on the scroll-work of its pilasters, the artist's only known work in that medium. The imported priest entered wearing a long silk mantle embroidered with a collage of texts printed in small capitals. I remembered that Saint Novellus was the patron of journalists.

I drove back to town and parked at L'Iris de Souss. As I entered the bar, a Chinese employee was exclaiming to Anna, "This man dump Suze on your greenery" as he pointed to a dripping philodendron. Shrugging her shoulders, the proprietress offered me a glass of the house apéritif. For lunch I contented myself with a single dish, the "Cocteau and Artaud," a brace of quenelles *à la ruthénoise*.

A passenger met aboard the *Haghion Pneuma*, the ship on which I had arrived the day before, joined me at the counter. It had been he who, standing next to me on the foredeck as we approached the town, named in order the peaks of the anfractuous range that rears its precipitous wall of pink limestone behind it: Mounts Pond, Souss (famous for its wild irises), Saint John…

"Is that N-n-noz over there?" I had asked, pointing to the highest eminence and repeating the one name cited in my cursory guidebook.

It was Mount Noz indeed. I asked if its summit was accessible by car. He said that a road existed, one too dilapidated for standard automobiles. However, a friend of his had invented a five-bladed fan that could be fitted to the underside of ordinary vehicles. Switched on, the fan, by blowing a concentrated air stream onto the road surface, created a cushion that allowed the chassis to pass safely and comfortably over any rut or pothole. Fan cars were available at local rental agencies; he recommended I try one. His friend, he added, was now at work on a new project: a writing car.

(I took his advice; but it was not until the last day of my quest that I made the ascent of Mount Noz. By then my third inquiry had ended in disappointment. With my last hope dashed, the excursion held little interest for me. At the top I found the usual observation platform and a telescope through which I examined the town and its surroundings, now bereft of all charm. My only consolation was finding a specimen of olive yarrow, Linnaeus's "forgotten plant.")

Now, at L'Iris, I learned that my shipboard companion was an Armenian recently established here. He had just traveled to Yerevan and had returned laden with periodicals to distribute among the Armenian community. Out of politeness I asked if his trip had gone smoothly. It had, he replied, except for "the usual Florence delay." He had had to change planes many times. When I suggested that a journey by sea might have been more direct, he flatly stated that such an option was inconceivable. He had taken the *Haghion Pneuma* only because the town was otherwise inaccessible. He related how, having fled to Lebanon after the 1917 massacres, his family had soon after embarked with him for Marseilles, only to have their ship founder three hours after leaving port. He had providentially survived, with his feet floating on a wooden bar stool and his head on one of his father's clogs, fashioned out of the dense *Taxus opacus* of Mount Ararat.

"In 1917?" I wondered. "Your age h-h-hardly—"

"I was three at the time." He looked a generation younger than his ninety-one years.

I telephoned the Lothar Schmidts: no answer. Driving to their house, I found it shuttered. I left the fan car at my hotel and wandered about the town until dark, then went back to L'Iris to return *The Quevedo Cipher* and choose a new book. Anna was behind the bar. I drank another Suze and, while chatting with her, told her of my supposed professional reasons for being here and my consequent disappointment at finding the Schmidts away.

"*She's* away — for some sort of psychotherapy," she told me. Anna evidently had known the couple well. She recounted, among other things, that Lothar Schmidt had recently left his mark on the history of medicine. He had locally and tentatively been diagnosed as suffering from a rare blood disorder called haemocrypsis. A sample of his blood had been sent to a specialized laboratory in Belgium, where, as part of one test, plasma had been injected into a young, healthy rabbit. Soon afterwards an altogether unexpected accident occurred: death intervened, "and in a way," Anna said, "that apparently makes it the only known instance of this type of death. I gather that in medical circles the case will henceforth be referred to as *the death from boredom.*"

"Of Sch-sch-schmidt?"

"The rabbit used in the test was the only animal left in the laboratory. The firm was in the process of moving from Bruges to Antwerp. All the mice, cats, and other rabbits had been taken to the new location. Alone, with only occasional human attention and nothing to do, watch, or listen to, the rabbit abruptly expired."

"And Schm... Schmidt?"

"He was cured by plenum acupuncture." Her attempted explanation of the treatment failed to enlighten me.

"What about M-m-m-mrs. Schmidt?"

Anna smiled and sighed. "Suki — a sweet lady. And in almost every way a respectable and respected one. For reasons she may discover on her present travels, she suffers from an irresistible attraction to Native Americans, especially from Latin America (although her 'depth champion,' as she defined him, hailed from Wyoming)." Since foreign commercial fleets began destroying the Peruvian fishing industry, Anna told me, more and more such Americans have sailed on ships that call here. First came the coastal Peruvians, then their mountain cousins, then *their* cousins from Ecuador and Bolivia. As soon as Suki heard that one had arrived, she would go down to the docks, find him, and lure him into bed, or even seduce him in some obscure warehouse corner. The owner of an in-and-out hotel near the port agreed to inform her when there was "her kind of flesh" ashore and of course — it was a very cahoots-cahoots relationship — to provide her with a room. The most notorious of her conquests was a young Ecuadorian from the hinterland. Like all his people, he wore a brass bell fastened to his throat by a leather thong. Suki caught him on the way back

S. ~~~~~~~~~~~

to his ship, led him into a nearby shed, and there cast off her wrap-around frock of Venetian lace, under which she was wearing nothing except her famous blue-cotton spider bra: at its points, circular holes let her nipples protrude; around each of them, eight furry stems radiated in an embroidered likeness of tarantula legs. Driven wild by this partial nakedness, the Ecuadorian did not wait to undress before taking her. The tolling of his thrusts could be heard all the way to the main square. Anna paused. "I have to add that the rumor that she publicly performs lapdances and other *cochonneries* to tempt her prey is unfounded. She has assured me that she reserves these practices for purely private encounters."

I asked what Suki looked like.

"Five foot eleven, blond — pure Scandinavian jock."

Anna suggested a restaurant. I took with me a copy of *Paul and Lulu*. (As I left, a German tourist was loudly complaining, "Boot I do not *like* booter!") I started the book at dinner. Returning to La Perla, I watched a group and young boys and girls rehearsing the *djerdan*, the time-honored festival dance. Two refrains I jotted down may catch something of its discreet lilt:

"Carmen"

"Medina"

I finished *Paul and Lulu* later that night. The novel tells the story of two charming, rather ineffectual con artists. They had only one consistently successful pat trick — "the veal caper." It permitted them, if not to prosper, at least to eat.

The following morning I woke up with a stiff neck and four bites from an out-of-season mosquito. I called up Pauline McDonald. Her gentle, weary voice, impossible to imagine as S's whatever her age, filled me with foreboding. I found her in the company of her daughter, a Mrs. Margarita Ford. She lived with the latter's family in a sprawling, modestly appointed apartment in the southern quarter. As I entered, broadcast presto strains of *Simone Boccanegra* were considerately hushed. One glance at Mrs. McDonald crushed any lingering expectation: portly, coarse, kindly — not a trace of a trace of a resemblance. She smelled of a cold cream my mother used long ago. I stayed perhaps fifteen minutes, long enough to lean that she had first come here to work as cook for a well-to-do local family. She had later continued to do sewing for them. She had had to quit their kitchen because the members of the household reserved their encounters in the dining room as occasions for sustained mutual vituperation; in time Mrs. McDonald could no longer bear seeing her best dishes grow cold under endless torrents of abuse. She had married Mr. McDonald — Willie, as she called him — when he had come here in retirement from his Cimmerian homeland. Just before I left, her chubby grandson entered, beaming proudly as he reported to his mother the results of his weekly weight review.

S. ~~~~~~~~~~~~

It was after this last, fruitless visit that I drove up Mount Noz. The fan car proved its worth. At an outdoor stand beside the parking area I lunched on a few gloom-ridden swallows of *duzhvo* (sp.?), a kind of cheeseless pizza. Such was my despondency and agitation that after lighting my last Flor de la Isabelita *cortado* I bit off and swallowed the first inch.

I drove down to the port and there booked passage on the *Haghion Pneuma*, scheduled to sail at midnight. At La Perla I packed my bags and paid my bill. I had nothing left to do but return *Paul and Lulu*.

In mid afternoon L'Iris was nearly empty. Anna was standing behind the bar with her back turned to me. She was dressed in a simple, flowing, astonishingly elegant black dress, one from a distant past. It was such a dress that Susanna had worn on that fateful evening thirty-seven years earlier, the last time I saw her. On the counter behind her were arrayed lengths of cord, a leather gag, packets no doubt containing mushroom powders. At that moment, presumably catching sight of me in the bottle-lined mirror, she curtly spoke:

"Miller!"

She placed her left hand on her crown and slowly lifted above her head a wig of blue-tinged, frilly hair. As she turned, long, full strands of silvered brunette fell about her perfect ears. Dropping the wig, she raised a thumb to each eye. Brown contact lenses popped into the dusky air, revealing unfathomable blueness.

The scales fell from my own eyes. I understood, not only

that "Souss" and "Suze" belonged to "Anna" and that a Schmidt might be known by his forge, but that I had nothing to forgive, nothing to punish. She was her own atonement: even if she had never been mine, I was hers. As she stepped from behind the bar I began trembling, the stammer points burned inwards from the base of my skull, I opened my mouth and made no sound.

She stretched her arms towards me: "Miller, you dodo! I never knew you cared."

About the Authors

FLORENCE DELAY, a resident of Paris, is the author of some two dozen books, including the novels *Riche et légère*, *Course d'amour pendant le deuil*, and *Etxemendi*.

PATRICK DEVILLE's novels include *Cordon bleu*, *Longue-vue*, *Femme parfaite*, and *Feu d'artifice*. He makes his home in Saint-Brevin, France.

JEAN ECHENOZ's works in English translation are *Cherokee* (winner of the Prix Médicis), *Double Jeopardy*, *Plan of Occupancy*, and *Big Blondes*. A recipient of the European Literature Prize for his novel *Lac*, he lives in Paris.

SONJA GREENLEE, who lives in Florida, has published fiction in various periodicals, and has recently completed her first novel.

HARRY MATHEWS's works include *The Conversions*, *Tlooth*, *The Sinking of the Odradek Stadium*, *Cigarettes*, and *The Journalist*, as well as many volumes of short fiction, poetry, and criticism. He divides his time between France and the United States.

MARK POLIZZOTTI lives near Boston, and is the author of *Revolution of the Mind: The Life of André Breton*, *Lautréamont Nomad*, and numerous translations.

OLIVIER ROLIN has published many works of fiction and travel reportage, including the novels *Bar des Flots Noirs*, *L'Invention du monde*, and *Port Soudain*. He lives in Paris.

MATTHEW ESCOBAR is a translator and novelist who lives near Paris.